GENTLEMEN PREFER . . . BRUNETTES

Nick Jefferson can't resist a challenge, or a blonde! So when the latest platinum-haired woman to cross his path challenges him to cook her a romantic dinner, he accepts. Unfortunately Nick could burn water . . . Chef Cassie Cornwell is *Not* Nick's type — she's a brunette, and the only woman to turn Nick down. She's disappointed he wants her to prepare a seduction feast rather than to share one. Unless Cassie can persuade him that blondes aren't necessarily more fun . . .

LIZ FIELDING

GENTLEMEN PREFER . . . BRUNETTES

Complete and Unabridged

LINFORD
Leicester

First published in Great Britain in 1998

First Linford Edition
published 2009

All the characters in this book have no existence
outside the imagination of the author, and have no
relation whatsoever to anyone bearing the same
name or names. They are not even distantly in-
spired by any individual known or unknown to the
author, and all the incidents are pure invention.

British Library CIP Data

Fielding, Liz.
    Gentlemen prefer - - brunettes. - -
    (Linford romance library)
    1. Love stories.
    2. Large type books.
    I. Title II. Series
    823.9'14—dc22

ISBN 978–1–84782–674–9

Published by
F. A. Thorpe (Publishing)
Anstey, Leicestershire

Set by Words & Graphics Ltd.
Anstey, Leicestershire
Printed and bound in Great Britain by
T. J. International Ltd., Padstow, Cornwall

This book is printed on acid-free paper

For wonderful aunts and uncles, with whom I have been much blessed.

1

Cassandra Cornwell had a problem. Or rather she had three of them, all male. Added to that, she was suffering from writer's cramp, smile fatigue and a serious lack of caffeine.

She looked up, hoping to catch Beth's eye, but her friend was too busy flinging herself into the arms of a man who had just walked through the door to notice her plight.

'Nick, darling!'

Beth's squeal of pleasure turned every head in the shop and Cassie paused mid-signature as 'Nick, darling' bent from his considerable height to kiss Beth's cheek.

The movement sent a thick cowlick of hair the colour of clear dark honey sliding over a broad, tanned forehead. 'Beth, you look gorgeous.' His voice was honey too — warm honey, running with butter over thick crunchy toast. 'I don't know why I ever let you get away.'

The squeal of pleasure, Cassie decided, had been thoroughly justified. The man was sex on a pair of very long legs, with a smile that fanned around a pair of dark eyes that she could tell, even from this distance, would make any woman feel beautiful, desired. The kind of man any girl would be a fool to take seriously.

Beth clearly knew that. 'There were just too many distractions, I guess,' she said, laughing. 'Let's see. There was Janine Grey . . . Georgia Thompson . . . Caroline Clifford — ' she ticked off the names on her fingers ' — and rumour had it that Diana Morgan . . . '

'Enough, Beth! Enough!' 'Nick, darling' held his hands up in mock surrender. 'I've never denied it. I just have this incurable weakness for tall blondes.'

'Tall, beautiful, *willowy* blondes,' Beth said, somewhat pointedly, as he hugged her own full curves. 'It's a

2

weakness that will get you into big trouble one of these days.'

'Is that a promise?'

'You are appalling, Nick. When are you going to grow up?'

His grin was an admission that Beth was right. But he wasn't contrite, far from it. 'Never, I hope. How's Harry?'

'Harry, bless him, is content with a tubby redhead. Long may it continue.'

'Not tubby, Beth. Deliciously curvaceous,' Nick murmured.

Beth snorted. Cassandra felt like snorting too. You could have too much honey. 'You'll never change. But mark my words, some woman will steal that playboy heart of yours one of these days. Just when you're least expecting it.'

'Common gossip has it that I don't have a heart to steal, Beth.'

'I know, but who listens to common gossip?' She linked her arm through his and gave it a squeeze. 'Is this a social call, darling, or are you buying?'

'I'm looking for a present for Helen;

it's her birthday next week. I saw you had a celebrity book signing . . . '

Nick Jefferson glanced across at the table piled high with books and found himself being soaked up by a pair of butterscotch eyes, eyes that were regarding him with the kind of look more usually bestowed upon a naughty puppy. Exasperated and trying very hard to be firm. But not quite making it.

Any sensible puppy worth a chocolate button would simply have rolled over and offered his tummy to be tickled. Nick wasn't a puppy so he contented himself with crossing the shop for a closer look.

He'd been on his way into the office when he'd noticed the poster announcing that Cassandra Cornwell, celebrated television cook, would be signing copies of her new book that day between eleven and twelve o'clock. He'd sent his secretary down at eleven, but she'd come back saying the place was mobbed and she'd go back later. But later she'd been rushing to get out some figures for him.

He could have called Beth and asked her to have a signed copy put by for him, but it occurred to him that if she was *that* busy it wouldn't be kind to drag her away to take a phone call when he was just a few floors above her. So he'd come himself. He was rather glad he had.

If he'd thought about Cassandra Cornwell he might have expected some middle-aged matron with red cheeks, greying hair and a slightly bossy manner. But she was none of those things. She had clear translucent skin, thick, glossy brows, eyes that smiled even when they were trying not to and dark, lustrous hair that was escaping her attempts to pin it tidily away from her face.

And she had the sweetest mouth. Like her eyes, it seemed to smile all by itself and he had this disconcerting urge to kiss it, certain that it would taste exactly like the strawberries he'd stolen from his mother's kitchen garden as a boy.

'. . . and you know how she loves to cook,' he finished, slowly.

'I'm not sure that I'd want a cookery book for my birthday,' Beth was saying as she followed him across the store. 'But heck, I'm not above parting a customer from his money, especially one as well endowed with the stuff as you. Cassie, do you know Nick Jefferson?' Behind his back she silently pointed upwards at the office block rising above them, indicating that he was *that* Jefferson.

Cassie tried to keep a straight face as Beth continued her pantomime, pointing at her wedding ring and shaking her head and then doing a melodramatic death scene which Cassie took to mean that he was the kind of man a girl would die for.

Apparently sensing something was going on behind his back, Nick began to turn but Cassie swiftly stuck out her hand and said, 'No, we haven't met.'

'Why?' he said, enfolding her hand — there was no other word that described the way he took hold of it, Cassie decided. He enfolded it, very tenderly in his own. His long, cool fingers seemed to reach up to her wrist, their tips resting lightly against a pulse that was fluttering in a quite ridiculous way. 'If you live in Melchester . . . '

She blinked at the casual ease with which he flirted. 'It's a big place, Mr Jefferson.' And she avoided the social circuit.

'Nick,' he urged.

'Nick, this is Cassandra Cornwell, a woman whose pastry could break your heart. She catered for my wedding, met a television researcher my brother was dating at the time and the rest is history.'

He glanced back at Beth, now fully recovered from her dramatic rendition of Nick Jefferson's bachelor status and leaning against the cash desk. 'History?'

'Television history. Cassie has the biggest television ratings for a cookery programme in the history of broadcasting. Women watch her programmes to learn how to cook the way their mothers used to. Men watch her television programmes and drool.' She gave Nick a thoughtful look. 'It may be her sticky toffee pudding that attracts them, but somehow I don't think so.'

'No, I don't think so either.'

'She's just come back to Melchester to live.'

'Lucky Melchester.' Despite the fact that she was at least six inches short of his gold standard and, like Beth, her figure leaned towards cuddly rather than super-model slender, Cassandra Cornwell, he decided, was exactly the kind of woman a man might fantasise about finding in his kitchen at the end of a hard day at the office. Warm, comforting, homely. Someone to massage your neck and put a drink in your hand to keep you happy until she served a meal fit for the gods. In short, the kind of girl a man would marry just to keep her all to himself. Not his type at all, in fact. Except for those lips.

Cassie, very much afraid that she had been doing a little drooling on her own account, swallowed and smiled politely. 'Hello, Nick.'

It was her cue for him to release her hand. He ignored it. Beneath her neat white shirt Cassie was uncomfortably aware that her skin was beginning to tingle dangerously and she threw a silent plea for rescue in Beth's direction, but her friend had been buttonholed by a customer and was disappearing towards the rear of the shop. And Nick Jefferson was showing no inclination to surrender her hand as her cheeks and quite a lot else began to heat up.

Maybe that was why he reached out and with just the tip of his finger touched the corner of her mouth. Maybe why, when she was still too startled, shaken, entranced to move away from this unexpected gesture, this most gentle of touches, he leaned forward and kissed her.

It was quite shocking. She should

have been shocked. He was a total stranger . . . well, not *total* exactly, they had been introduced . . . and they were in the middle of a classy bookshop in the atrium of a very classy high-rise building. She should have stopped him; she knew it. The trouble was, it just wasn't the kind of kiss that a girl wanted to stop. Ever.

He didn't seem in too much of a hurry to bring it to an end, either. His lips moved over hers lightly, inquisitively, as if he was seeking out something rare and precious. And when finally he did stop she heard herself give a little, regretful sigh.

That was when she realised with horror that she was the one actively seeking to prolong the kiss, her face lifted invitingly, her lips slightly parted. She snapped her eyes open to see Nick Jefferson regarding her with the dark, knowing eyes of a man used to making instant conquests.

'I was right,' he said, before she could ask him what the hell he thought he was doing. Actually, he sounded surprised, which threw her a little.

'Right . . . ?' Cassie began, distracted from her legitimate indignation. Then, realising that she was still looking up at him in a way that almost begged him to kiss her again, she made a determined effort to pull herself together. 'Right about what?' she demanded, straightening and attempting to retrieve her hand, but he was having none of that.

Aware that several people had stopped browsing amongst the shelves and turned to stare at them, she allowed her fingers to remain in his. Rather than provoke an unseemly struggle. At least that was what she told herself she was doing. But somewhere, at the back of her mind, there was the faint sound of hollow laughter.

'I was right about your mouth,' he said. 'It tastes of strawberries.'

Strawberries! Cassie was very much afraid that the blush had finally materialised beneath the twin assaults of his touch and the intensity of his gaze. And she was furious with herself. The man was an incorrigible flirt; he probably couldn't help himself but that was no reason to encourage him.

'Really?' she enquired, her voice considerably cooler than her body, which was pounding from the jolt of sexual awareness provoked by his touch. She had forgotten that sudden, unexpected collision of desire when a stranger reached for your hand. Or maybe she'd just been avoiding it for such a long time that she had fooled herself into believing that it would never happen again . . .

Whichever it was, she told herself firmly, she was too old to be taken in by such an obvious pass. He was just doing it to impress Beth. Except that Beth was nowhere to be seen. Whatever. He was impressing the hell out of her and that would never do. 'Strawberries?' she repeated, thoughtfully. 'What variety of strawberries?'

If she had hoped to crush him with this put-down, she was doomed to disappointment. His eyes crinkled into a slow, wide and infinitely seductive smile. 'The small sweet ones that are bright red all the way through,' he murmured. 'The kind that when you squash one between your fingers it dribbles dark red juice into your mouth.'

'Oh.' The image evoked was so sensuous, so real that Cassie sincerely wished she hadn't asked. But at least he had surrendered her hand, finally.

Her reprieve was short-lived, however, since he used the hand to hitch an inch or two of expensive lightweight suiting over his knee and prop himself on the edge of the table at which she was sitting. Then he leaned across her to pick up one of her glossy new cookery books.

She steeled herself against the warm man-scent of freshly laundered linen, soap and an elusive trace of the kind of cologne they didn't sell in the local supermarket. Nick Jefferson, on the other hand, began idly flipping through the pages as if nothing had happened. Seriously tempted to take it from him and hit him with it, she restrained herself. It would undoubtedly be wisest to follow his example and pretend that nothing had.

Easier said than done. Her lips were singing from his delicate touch and she found herself wondering what it would be like to have Nick Jefferson hold her face between those long, sensitive fingers and kiss her seriously. Then she wondered if she was going quite mad.

'I'm sure Helen will love this,' he said, making her jump.

'Helen?'

'My sister,' he told her.

'Oh, yes, of course.' Again that knowing smile as if he had sensed the ridiculous flash of jealousy at the mention of another woman's name. Lord, but the man was arrogant. And she was an idiot.

'Well, far be it from me to discourage you from buying a copy of my book, but I'm rather inclined to agree with

Beth. It's hardly the kind of present a girl expects for her birthday.'

'Well, this is just a little extra. Helen loves to cook — she collects new cookery books the way some women collect jewels. She's a great fan of yours — which is why I came in when I saw the poster. Now I've met you, I can understand why.'

Cassie ignored the smooth compliment. She strongly doubted that he had ever heard of her and she was positive that he was not the kind of man to waste time discussing cookery with his sister.

'I think I'd rather buy my own cookery books and have someone give me jewels for my birthday,' she said feelingly.

'Don't worry, Cassandra, I'll find her some exciting surprise to go with it. I'm not that cheap.'

No. She'd never thought he would be cheap. On the contrary, she was certain that he was a man who would be overwhelmingly generous with the little treasures that money could buy. But something warned her that he would be as mean as Scrooge with anything as important as emotional commitment.

'Would you like me to sign it for her?' she asked, holding out her hand to take the book, but he was apparently in no great hurry, turning the book towards her so that she could see the picture he had been looking at.

'Sussex Pond Pudding?' he queried, eyebrows raised just a fraction. 'Is that for real?'

Cassie was not convinced by his apparent interest in recipes, certain that he had further dalliance on his mind. But she was determined not to be drawn into further flirtation with a man who obviously thought he was irresistible — who quite probably was irresistible to anyone looking for a meaningless flirtation. But that was not her. However, she had to clear her throat before she could attain sufficient briskness to answer him.

'Have you never tried it? It's a

traditional English pudding,' she explained, as if lecturing a class of fourteen-year-olds at the local comprehensive. 'The pond is a lemon and butter sauce that forms a moat around the pudding when it's turned out of its basin. It's loaded with calories, of course — but it is quite delicious. Maybe,' she added, 'if the surprise is exciting enough, your sister will make it for you.'

'Maybe she will,' he acknowledged, continuing to flip through the book. 'And what about fluffs and fools and flummeries?' he enquired, stopping at a page near the end of the book. 'Are they stuffed with calories too?'

She shrugged. 'They're certainly stuffed with cream.'

He closed the book with a little snap and turned it over. 'Maybe you should print a health warning on the cover.' He raised the book slightly as once more his smile deepened the creases around his mouth, sending tiny crinkled fans out from the corners of his eyes.

'They're also full of good fresh fruit.

Have you never heard the expression that a little of what you fancy does you good, Nick?'

'Certainly. It's a philosophy I subscribe to most heartily. But not necessarily in regard to food. Besides, I thought it was all low-fat, no-added-sugar that did you good these days?'

Cassie discounted the smile. There was no denying that the man was gorgeous, but he was just a little too aware of the fact. Besides, she wasn't a tall, willowy blonde so he was presumably just using her to practise on until something more to his taste came along.

'Frankly, I'd rather go without. And no one is suggesting you eat them every day. You can have too much of a good thing, particularly flummery,' she said pointedly.

'Is that a particularly rich dish?' he asked, a touch dangerously.

Coming from him it was; the glint of mischief in his eyes betrayed him. She was quite certain he was aware that the word had another meaning, one that he would be far more familiar with . . . nonsense, humbug, empty trifling.

Beth, who had dealt with her customer, returned in time to witness the sudden flush of bright pink spots that had appeared on Cassie's cheeks. 'If you think flummery is rich, my friend, you should try Cassie's toad-in-the-hole,' she interjected hurriedly.

'Should I?' Nick asked, continuing to look straight down into Cassie's eyes. 'If I catch the toad will you cook it for me?'

'Buy yourself a copy of the book, Nick,' Beth advised him. 'It will be an investment. One day you'll run out of women to charm and then you'll have to learn to cook for yourself.'

'I've never charmed a woman for her talents in the kitchen, Beth,' he said, without taking his gaze from Cassie. 'This town is full of good restaurants.' He hadn't missed the hectic colour that had seared her cheekbones, confirming that despite her very cool manner he was making some kind of impression on Miss Cassandra Cornwell. Quite what kind of impression he wasn't sure, which was unusual enough in itself to interest him. 'But I'll buy one if Cassie will inscribe it for me.'

'Of course she will,' Beth said, suddenly businesslike. 'What would you like her to write?'

'Oh, I'll leave that to Cassie. I'm sure she'll think of something appropriate,' he said, offering her the book.

'How about, 'To Nick Jefferson, the most accomplished — ?''

'The most accomplished cook in town,' Nick completed, cutting Beth off before she could say something completely outrageous.

'But you can't cook,' Cassie reminded him, with excessive politeness. Nick had a feeling that she would have preferred to throw one of her cookery books at him. A whole pile of books, perhaps. He rather thought he would like to see her try.

'Won't your book teach me how to

turn out perfect meals in minutes?' he asked, provoking her some more. 'That is the dream you're peddling?'

'On the contrary. Anyone can heat up some fancy cook-chill meal from the supermarket these days.' She laid her hand on the pile of books beside her. 'I write about the kind of old-fashioned cooking that takes time and love to produce. My readers cook for pleasure, Nick, and so do I, not for the instant gratification of fast food.'

'I can see why your television show is so popular, Cassandra. Nostalgia is really big right now.'

'Don't you sometimes long for a taste of rice pudding the way your mother made it? With butter and sultanas and freshly grated nutmeg?'

'No, I always preferred fresh picked strawberries. And if the strawberries were stolen . . . '

He wasn't talking about puddings any more. 'That's nostalgia too,' Cassie interrupted, just a touch crossly. 'And what about the dreams you're selling?'

She indicated the floors above her, the glass tower of Jefferson Sports headquarters, glistening in the summer sunshine, dominating the town. 'Buy this great new tennis racquet, or these expensive golf clubs, and you too can be the world champion? Where's the reality in that?'

Beth choked. Neither of them noticed.

'Not world champion.' He lifted one corner of his mouth in the kind of smile that would have had most women gasping for more. '*Club* champion, maybe. But Jefferson Sports sells more than one kind of dream. We sell the great outdoors, too. Camping gear, fishing rods, hiking and sports equipment, in fact the complete antidote to over-indulgence in your kind of cooking.'

'You'll be needing a tent, won't you, Cassie?' Beth put in swiftly, before things got totally out of hand. 'If you ask him nicely, I'm sure Nick will show you his entire range.' She paused, a wicked little twinkle appearing in her eyes. 'You never know, he might even offer to pitch it for you.'

'Are you going camping?' he asked Cassie.

'You bet she is,' Beth said, answering for her. 'In fact she's going with three perfectly adorable young men.'

'Boys,' Cassie muttered, refusing to allow Beth to make something out of this stupid flirtation. 'And I already have a tent.'

'Three boys?' He glanced at her ringless hand, not that it meant anything these days . . . 'Yours?' he asked.

'My nephews. They want a taste of the big outdoors and since my sister and her husband are going away for a week I volunteered to take them.'

'Just you and three boys? Beth could be right. You'll need someone who knows what he's doing to put up the tent.'

'Will I? Is it that difficult?'

'A nightmare if you don't know what you're doing.'

'Do you warn your customers about that when you're selling them one of your dream tents?'

23

'We do advise them to have a practice run at home in the garden before they go trekking up the Amazon. Have you done that, Miss Cornwell?'

'Trekked up the Amazon?'

'Had a practice run — in the garden?'

'Not yet.'

'You should. This weather isn't going to hold for ever. It might be pouring with rain, or blowing a force ten gale when you get to wherever you're going.'

'Are you volunteering to show me how it's done, Mr Jefferson?' She didn't think so. He was doing it on automatic, Cassie decided. It wasn't anything personal; he wasn't in the least bit interested in her, he just couldn't help himself.

'Maybe. Why don't we discuss it over lunch?'

Lunch? The man really was too much. Did he think she would swoon into his arms with gratitude?

'Won't you be too busy pursuing leggy blondes to worry about me and three small boys?' she enquired, keeping the edge from her voice with difficulty as, determined to put an end to this nonsense, she turned to the flyleaf of the book.

'Who said I pursued anyone?'

The implication being that they pursued him? Good grief. 'Your sister's name is Helen, I think you said?' She refused to take any further part in this conversation.

'That's right.' She signed the book, handed it to Beth to wrap and waited for him to go. He didn't. 'Don't forget my book, Cassandra,' he reminded her.

She'd assumed his offer to buy a book had been simply part of the game — in fact she'd been sure it was. But if he had more money than sense she wasn't about to argue. She took a second book from the pile, opened it and for a moment considered the bare white space of the flyleaf.

Then she wrote, 'For Nick Jefferson — a man to be taken with just a pinch of salt.' Then she signed it and handed it to him.

2

Nick regarded the inscription for a moment before passing the book to Beth with his charge card without comment. A man had to pay for his pleasure, after all, and flirting with Cassandra Cornwell had certainly been different. Whether he could describe it entirely as a pleasure he couldn't be sure. Except for that kiss. He hadn't been kidding about the strawberries.

'Now, where shall we have lunch?' he asked Cassie. 'I'm sure you know all the best places.'

Not as well as he did; she was certain of that. 'I'm sorry, Nick, I already have a luncheon engagement.' She offered him her hand without thinking . . . at least, she hoped she hadn't been thinking. 'I do hope your sister enjoys the book.'

'And what about me?' He was

holding onto her hand again, the pad of his thumb pressed against the backs of her fingers in something close to a caress. Cassie retrieved it quickly. She was twenty-seven years old, well beyond the point in life where she was prepared to become just another entry in any man's little black book.

'You'll never open your book again,' she said briskly. 'You'll just stick it on a shelf somewhere, or maybe it won't even get that far. Maybe you'll just go back to your office and give it to your secretary.'

'Not with that inscription, I won't.'

'You didn't think it appropriate? I'm sorry, Nick. Would you like me to give you your money back?'

'No.' Then, as she reached for her bag, he added, 'I can't wait to read it more closely.'

'Nonsense. You'll hide it away in the bottom drawer of your desk and forget all about it. That would be such a waste when I can find a good home for it.' She opened her purse and began to extract the money to refund the cost of the book.

Nick closed his hand over hers. 'Put your money away. I promise I shall take your book home with me this evening and study it with the closest interest. Who knows? Maybe you'll convert me and I'll be tempted to cook something.'

'Be careful you don't make a complete strawberry fool of yourself, Nick,' Beth warned him as she returned his card and handed him the books in a bag. 'Give my best wishes to your mother and don't wait for Helen's next birthday before you drop in again. You do have to pass the door every day,' she reminded him.

'I won't,' he promised, his gaze lingering momentarily on Cassie. Then he stepped through the door and out into the huge airy atrium that rose through the centre of the building.

'Whew!' Cassie said, flopping back in her chair as the door swung shut behind him. And she shook her fingers, blowing on her nails as if scorched.

Beth laughed. 'You're a cool one, Cassie. I should think it's a totally new experience for Nick to be turned down for anything, particularly lunch in some fancy restaurant.'

'Then I shall take comfort in the certainty that the experience will be a memorable one for him.' She smiled slightly. 'Which is more than can be said for the dish of the day — which is all I would have been if I'd said yes.'

'I see your point. So who are you lunching with?'

'You. My treat.'

'You turned down Nick Jefferson for me? Lady, you need to get your priorities right.'

'Just because the man makes me sizzle, Beth, doesn't mean I have to leap onto the plate and hand him the mustard.'

'He does make you sizzle, then?'

'Only in the same way as your average movie star.'

'Oh?'

'You know. You go to the cinema and

while the lights are down he's all yours. Then you go home. Men are safer that way.'

'Don't you find safety a touch boring?'

'Not at all. Besides, you heard the man. He has an incurable weakness for blondes.'

'I know. Tall blondes at that. The cool Grace Kelly type. One has just taken up residence in the Jefferson Sports marketing department and I hear the guys are laying odds on how long it will take her to succumb to the Jefferson charm. But do you know something? For all the lovely blondes Nick's chased and undoubtedly caught in the last few years, he's never actually been tempted to marry one of them. Doesn't that tell you something?'

'That they're smart?'

'You're not that cynical, Cassie.'

'Oh, yes, I am.' The onlooker saw more of the game and she'd been an onlooker for long enough to know that she'd made the right decision. But she was human enough to be interested in a little hot gossip. 'He's never even come close?' she asked.

Beth shrugged. 'He bought a lovely cottage just outside town a few years back and everyone got excited about that, assuming he was going to take the plunge.'

'And?'

'It turned out he was having fun with an interior decorator at the time. I suppose she just wanted something to practise on and he was inclined to indulge her. Once she'd finished with the cottage she moved on.' She grinned. 'Or maybe he moved her on.'

'That sounds more likely. After all, why would he bother to marry anyone when he's having such a good time?'

Beth frowned. 'Nick isn't like that.'

'No?' Cassie shook her head. 'He's a good-looking man, Beth, and maybe he's as nice as you say, but I like a little more bottom to a man.'

'Bottom? He has the cutest butt — '

'Substance. *Gravitas*,' Cassie interrupted

quickly. 'Nick Jefferson is a cuckoo. A very charming, very beguiling cuckoo, no doubt, and I can see the way your mind is working. But I'm a swan — so don't even think about it.'

Beth's forehead wrinkled up into a frown. 'A swan?'

'They mate for life.' It was an excuse that had served her well enough until now, but her fingers strayed to lips still tingling from that unexpected kiss. Then she saw Beth looking at her with an expression that mingled sympathy with just a touch of exasperation, a look that said five years was long enough to mourn for anyone. 'I know, I'll probably end my days talking to my cat,' she said, quickly, before Beth said it for her.

'Possibly, but that's no reason not to have a little fun with the cuckoos, or even the ducks, while you're waiting for another swan to come along. I imagine swans do look for another mate if the first one ... It's not too late to call Nick back and tell him you've changed your mind about lunch — ' She began to move towards the door.

'Stay right where you are, Beth Winslet. Nick Jefferson is not my kind of man.'

'He's every girl's kind of man,' Beth said with a grin.

'Exactly. And he isn't about to saddle himself with one when he can have the whole gallery, now is he? So, where am I going to take you for lunch?'

Beth continued to challenge her for another thirty seconds, then she threw up her hands, conceding defeat. 'I should be treating you,' she said. 'I can't believe the number of people you brought into the shop this morning.'

'And some of them even bought a book,' Cassie said with a grin as she signed the books left on the table.

'I know you hate these things. It was good of you to give up your morning.'

'It was the least I could do. After all, catering for your wedding changed my life — '

'Lunch with Nick Jefferson might well have done the same,' Beth pointed out. 'Have you ever considered the possibility that I might be your fairy godmother — ?'

'You're not suggesting that Nick Jefferson is Prince Charming?'

'Heaven forbid. I wouldn't wish Prince Charming on any woman. Just consider ... He lined up all the beauties in the land so that he could take his pick of them. And then he chose Cinderella by the size of her feet. How sad can you get?'

'Well, when you put it like that ... '

'I do. I have to admit that you do have the daintiest little feet I've ever seen — but I have the feeling that Nick looks for a little more than that in a woman.'

'Blonde hair, super-model looks?' Cassie suggested.

'Well, what do men know? As your fairy godmother my advice would have been to let him take you to lunch.'

'I'd advise you to hang up your wand and quit while you're ahead, Beth. Now, I've discovered this great little place down by the river. So, what do you say?'

'Thank you?'

'That'll do nicely.'

★ ★ ★

Twenty floors above them in the Jefferson Tower, Nick Jefferson was facing a problem of his own. She was approaching him right now across the marble floor of the lobby. Tall, slender, with platinum hair that emphasised her glacial beauty, Veronica Grant was a distinctly superior female and since she'd been brought in as a consultant to work with the marketing department she'd had every man who worked at the headquarters of Jefferson Sports drooling over her every word, even the ones old enough and married enough to know better.

Not that she gave them any encouragement. Professional to her fingertips, she confined her conversation strictly to the job in hand. She appeared to be quite unaware of the testosterone rampaging in her wake as she walked through the building.

Appeared to be. Nick Jefferson was not entirely convinced about that. There wasn't a woman yet born *that* oblivious of the ripples she caused as she walked across a room. Not when the ripples were of tidal-wave proportions. It had to be an act. Didn't it?

The temptation to find out was almost irresistible. After all, his name headed the list of odds in the 'Ice Queen Stakes' that some clown had posted in the men's room — hardly surprising in view of the fact that his family owned the business and that he was still, despite his thirty-three years, one of the few men on the list without at least one failed marriage behind him. A situation he was in no hurry to change. He'd seen the bitter aftermath of too many marriages that had ended on the rocks to be eager to rush into wedlock.

Not that his name seemed to impress

Veronica Grant. She treated him with the same rather distant politeness that she bestowed on everyone else.

He wondered if she knew about the list. He'd ordered its removal the moment he'd seen it, well aware that the female thought-police of the typing pool would pounce on such political incorrectness with glee. But things like that had a way of getting around; which meant that simply asking her out to dinner the way he might any other new colleague was likely to be met with a certain amount of suspicion. He was well aware that more than one of his colleagues had made the mistake of being too eager. Her response had been a polite but definite 'No, thank you'. No excuse. No face-saving suggestion that she was busy, or involved with someone else. Just a plain, unadorned 'no'.

Was it just that she didn't mix business with pleasure? he wondered. Or was she waiting for something better to come along? The heir apparent to the

Jefferson Sports empire, for instance?

Veronica nodded as she fell in beside him at the lifts. 'Hello, Nick.' That was about as personal as her conversation got.

'Veronica,' he returned distractedly, stepping into the lift ahead of her, well aware that she would take instant offence at any suggestion of patronising deference to the weaker sex. Apparently she didn't subscribe to the concept of a weaker sex and he was pretty sure that she could teach the typing pool a thing or two about PC behaviour.

'What's up, Nick? You look as if you're about to report a slump in the sales figures.'

'Do I?' He didn't allow his triumph at this small breakthrough to show, merely looked slightly puzzled. Then he said, 'Oh, no. It's my sister's birthday next week. I've just bought her a cookery book — '

'I saw Cassandra Cornwell had a signing.'

'Yes, well, that's the predictable gift.

Now I've got to think of something special as a surprise.'

'Send her a cheque.'

'A cheque?' That would certainly fulfil the surprise element. It surprised the hell out of him. 'Isn't that a bit . . . impersonal?'

'But easy. And it saves time, postage and footwear. Believe me, it's a great deal more enjoyable getting an impersonal cheque than being presented with something you'd be ashamed to put in the garbage.'

Her bluntness was refreshing, even if her assessment of his taste was less than flattering. But it was the longest conversation they'd had on any subject other than marketing in the three weeks since she'd moved into the office opposite his. Maybe he could string it out a little further, learn a little about her likes and dislikes.

'It's a tempting idea, but I don't think it would go down too well with Helen. Kid sisters like to be spoiled a little, you know.'

'Do they?' She gave him a long, assessing glance from a pair of silvery blue eyes. 'She can't be that much of a kid.'

He shrugged. This was one hard female. Here he was, a warm, caring brother, worrying about a gift for his sister, and was this woman impressed? Would anything impress her? An uneasy feeling that it might be wiser to ignore the challenge on the men's room wall abruptly hardened into determination to see just what it would take to soften her heart.

It wasn't as if it would be a hardship, exactly. He considered the perfection of seemingly endless legs, the slender figure expensively clad in cool ice-blue linen that so exactly matched her character, the smooth platinum curve of hair. The contrast with the vivid, inviting warmth of Cassie Cornwell couldn't have been more marked.

'I suppose not,' he conceded quickly, before his thoughts ran away with him. Dimpled little pouter pigeons were not his style. He'd always liked his women to have the lines of a well-bred greyhound. 'Helen's got four of her own.'

'Four? *Four children?*'

If he'd suggested sex in the lift she couldn't have been more shocked. 'She started young,' he explained. 'And last time she had twins.'

'In that case forget the cheque, just take her children off her hands for the weekend and give the poor woman a break.'

He laughed out loud. 'Four girls? You've got to be joking.'

'Have I?' Veronica's voice maintained its neutral tone, giving nothing away. 'I'd have thought four girls would have been right up your street.'

Nick opened his mouth to protest at this calumny, but decided that might not be a wise move. The grapevine had obviously been busily filling her in on the details of his bachelor existence. So he grinned instead. 'Not four girls between the ages of five and eight,

Veronica.' And he found his thoughts drifting to Cassandra Cornwell. She was taking her nephews camping. He was assailed with a sudden vision of her waking up early, stretching and then curling back into the warmth of her sleeping bag like a dormouse . . .

'Well, I'm sure a man of your experience will think of some treat to take the poor woman's mind off runny noses for a few minutes, Nick,' Veronica said, breaking into his thoughts. 'Some way to light up her day.'

He dragged himself back from the enticing thought of curling up with Cassie and gave his full attention to Veronica. Poor woman? It was the second time in as many minutes that she'd referred to his sister in that condescending manner. He'd like to see her try it to Helen's face; she'd soon be put in her place.

Just because his sister thought her family was more important than running a company, that didn't mean she couldn't do both if she'd a mind to.

Probably with one hand tied behind her back. Even surrounded by boxes of nappies and baby goo she had found time to train for and compete in the London Marathon. And turn in one of the fastest amateur times. Her role as wife and mother might be her first priority but she was still a Jefferson. However, Helen didn't need him or anyone else to stand up for her, so he let it go.

'I'm sure you're right, Veronica,' he said as the lift door opened. 'I'll think of something. Every woman has a weak spot.' And he'd find hers, he promised himself, and sooner rather than later.

As for Helen, Veronica might have inadvertently offered a solution. Not a cheque — because despite all the advantages Veronica had outlined he knew better than to send his sister money. Helen would return it with a reminder that money was something you gave to charity; sisters deserved a little more time and thought. But then sisters were notoriously blind to their brothers' good qualities, presumably because they'd lived with them through childhood and adolescence and had been the victim of all their worst ones.

That couldn't be Veronica Grant's problem, though. Not that he was entirely convinced by her arm's length tactics. She might be a very clever woman but he wasn't exactly stupid himself. He was number two at Jefferson Sports and when his uncle retired in a year or two he'd be number one. The Jefferson name and the money which went with it were a plum prize and he was well aware that he was a target for every matchmaking mama in Melchester.

If that was Veronica's game she was doomed to disappointment. A little kiss chase was one thing but he had no intention of getting involved in anything heavier. He was simply out to prove a point, not change his life. He liked his life just the way it was.

But he hated to walk away from a challenge. It ran in the blood. His grandfather had been a track hero, his father had played rugby for his country and his uncle had been about to follow him when he was sidelined by injury. The three of them had put Jefferson Sports on the map and expected their offspring to follow in their mighty footsteps.

While his cousins had taken to the professional sports field with enthusiasm, adding glory to the family name, Nick had chosen instead to flex his muscles in the business world. After all, someone had to stay home and mind the store. He'd done his bit for the family honour with a rowing blue for his university, but he'd long outgrown such gladiatorial contests. Not that he was a slouch on the tennis court, or the piste, but sport, in his book, was for fun. He particularly enjoyed the indoor kind.

He was smiling as he dropped the bookstore carrier bag on his desk and reached for the telephone to call his brother-in-law. But as he waited for a connection his gaze fell on the bright bag and his smile turned into a frown.

Cassandra Cornwell was not his kind of woman. Short, with an armful of curves and an uncontrollable mop of dark hair, she was the very antithesis of the kind of woman he liked to be seen with. He couldn't think why he had asked her to lunch. Or why he had been so irked when she had turned him down. Except that she reminded him of a little brown teddy bear he'd had as a child. Soft and warm . . . and cuddly. He suddenly realised that someone was speaking into his ear.

'Oh, Graham, it's Nick. I've just had a bright idea for Helen's birthday. How would you two like to spend it in Paris? On me?'

* * *

'Tell me about your nephews, Cassie,' Beth invited as they settled themselves in the small, elegant dining room overlooking the river. 'Why do you feel

46

you have to take them out into the wild woods and introduce them to nature in the raw? Surely that's their father's job?'

'Their father has something more important on his mind. And I don't mind, really.'

'Bravely spoken.'

'No, it'll be fun. They're great kids. I took them with me to an ice-cream factory a few weeks back and we had a ball. I'm more worried about the boys' parents than looking after their off-spring . . . ' Cassie shrugged. 'I'm pretty sure that my sister is having problems with her marriage. I know Lauren's sick to the back teeth of being left alone with the boys while Matt's been spending all the hours of the day and night working.'

'We all have to make sacrifices, Cassie. It's tough out there.'

'I know that. Lauren does too, I'm sure, but you know how it is. Tension starts to build up over something stupid and before you know it you're nursing

47

every grudge under the sun. I had lunch with them a few weeks back and frankly the place was like a powder keg on a dodgy fuse. Then, when Lauren found out that Matt had promised to take the boys away on a camping trip on the few days he was planning to take off this summer instead of spending the time with her on a proper family vacation . . . well . . . I had to do something . . . '

'So you volunteered to take over the camping trip? Single-handed? Couldn't you have bought the boys off with a trip to Disneyland Paris?'

'Matt's mother took them in the Easter holiday.'

'So?'

'Well, it would have looked a bit obvious.'

'And this doesn't?'

'I managed to convince them that I was planning a series on cooking outdoors . . . practically begged them to let me do it . . . ' Cassie smiled ruefully. 'You think I'm mad, don't you?'

'Actually, I think you're a peach. Mad, but a peach. But are you sure you're wise to go on your own?'

'Do you mean without a man to take care of me?' Cassie enquired dangerously.

'Well, it's always nice to have one handy. Even if it's only to pitch the tent and fetch the water.' Her eyes sparkled with mischief. 'And any other little job that needs doing.'

'Maybe I should have taken Nick up on his offer of lunch after all. Who knows where it might have led?'

Beth stopped scanning the menu long enough to laugh out loud. 'Oh, I'm sure you do. Just because you've chosen a life of celibacy doesn't mean that you've lost your memory.' She frowned. 'Or maybe it does.'

'You're not suggesting a double sleeping bag, are you, Beth?' Cassie responded in mock horror.

'I am, actually. But not just any double sleeping bag, you understand. I'm suggesting a top-of-the-range Jefferson Sports double duck-down sleeping bag.'

'Have another glass of wine and say that.'

Cassie's laughter turned the heads of several lunching businessmen. They were in no hurry to look away.

'Just think how romantic it would be, Cass, zipped up together beneath the stars.'

Cassie was trying not to think about it. She didn't understand why it was so hard. 'With three small boys playing gooseberry? I think I'd rather manage on my own, thanks. Unless, of course, you fancy a week of outdoor fun in the wilds of Wales? You'd be most welcome.'

'Me? I've got a store to run. Those cookery books and videos don't just sell themselves, you know.' Then she thought about it. 'Actually in your case they do. But someone has to take the money.' And to emphasise that she was not to be persuaded she returned to her close scrutiny of the menu. 'I'll have the lamb cutlets with the herb and mustard crust, baby new potatoes and peas,' she said, after reading it through twice.

'I can't tempt you to try the scallops, first?' Cassie asked innocently.

'Please! This is lunchtime. If I eat too much I'll fall asleep over the accounts.'

'You're quite sure? I've heard they're very special and I'd like to try them. If you don't mind waiting . . . '

'Sit and watch you eat?' Beth groaned. 'You wretch, you know I've got all the restraint of a rabbit faced with a field of lettuce.'

Cassie grinned. 'Save the lettuce for supper and join me in the gym tomorrow to work off the excess.'

Beth brightened. 'Oh, right. What time?'

'Six-thirty.'

'Six-thirty? Forget it. After a day in the bookshop all I can think of is a large G and T and putting my feet up.'

Cassie grinned. 'I meant six-thirty in the morning.'

Beth's mouth fell open, then she gathered herself, with the smallest of shudders. 'No, thanks. I'll learn to love my curves and if you don't mind my saying so you need a man to keep you in bed in the morning.' Even as she said it, Cassie saw Beth wish the words back into her mouth. 'As I said, the restraint of a rabbit and a mouth like a runaway train . . .'

3

Cassie took pity on her. 'Don't worry about it, Beth. You're only saying what everyone else thinks. Matt and Lauren have been trying to fix me up with their spare men friends for years.'

'Look, since this is apparently my day for saying the wrong thing, can I do it again?'

'Will anything stop you?'

'It's just that . . . well, has it ever occurred to you that Jonathan might not have been a swan after all? You'd only been married a few weeks when he died, hardly long enough to find out the faults. And they all have faults, you know. Even the best of them.'

'I know, Beth.'

'It's unfair to measure every man you meet against him.'

'I know.'

'But it doesn't make any difference?'

'Beth, you don't understand . . . '
The waitress arrived to take their order
and when she had gone the urge to tell
someone, anyone, the truth about
Jonathan had evaporated. That was her
secret. Her shame. 'Are you sure you
won't come along to the gym?'

'At six-thirty?' Beth seemed as
relieved to let the subject drop as she
was.

'An hour in the gym three mornings
a week helps to counteract the occupa-
tional hazard of constantly tasting new
recipes to get them just right.'

'You mean you claim membership of
the gym as an expense against income
tax?' Beth was seriously impressed by
that.

'I hadn't thought of it,' Cassie
confessed.

'Check it out with your accountant
and let me know what he says. I wonder
if I could get away with it? You have to
be fit to run your own business, you
know.'

'You have to be fit for any kind of job

and somehow I can't imagine the Inland Revenue subsidising health club membership for the entire nation.'

'Why not? Think what it would save on the National Health bill.'

'You know, you're wasted in business, Beth. With a mind like that you should be in politics. Running the Exchequer.'

* * *

'Are you coming, Nick? The meeting is about to start.'

Veronica was framed in the doorway, her slender figure displayed to advantage in the palest grey and white dress. Outside the day was hot and humid, yet this woman managed to look as if she was moving in her own air-conditioned space, a picture of unruffled poise. He suspected that if she were a glass she would be frosted. The very opposite of the way he was feeling at that moment.

'I'll be right with you,' he muttered, wishing she would move on instead of watching him hunt through the papers on his desk for a sheet of figures that had disappeared without trace.

Instead, she asked, 'Lost something?' in a tone that suggested a whole heap of things. But mostly that she had never lost anything in her entire life.

'One of my secretary's kids is sick,' he muttered. 'But I know she did those figures before she went home last night . . . '

Veronica appeared to glide across the room, then, bending from the knees, she picked up a sheet of paper that had fallen beneath his desk. 'Is this what you're looking for?' she enquired as she stood up and offered it to him, a faint smile lifting the corners of her mouth. Like everything she did it combined an economy of movement with perfect grace. He wondered briefly if she had ever been a model, but immediately discounted the possibility that she would ever involve herself in an occupation so trivial.

'That's it. Thanks, Veronica.' He smiled somewhat ruefully, raking his fingers through his hair. 'I seem to be all over the place today,' he said, with a slightly helpless shrug. That 'little boy lost' thing seemed to get to some women. Maybe it would touch Veronica Grant.

'The heat gets to some people.' Her tone suggested only the weak and feeble.

Obviously not.

He shuffled the papers into order and picked up the folder with the details of the new project he had been working on. Beneath it lay Cassie Cornwell's book, which, despite his promise, had not been opened since he bought it. But at least he hadn't hidden it away in the bottom of his desk as she had predicted. Veronica picked it up and turned it over to examine the photograph on the back.

'Is this the book you're giving your sister?' she asked.

'Yes . . . and no.' He shrugged. 'I bought more than one copy.'

Veronica's eyebrows moved upwards

in gentle query. 'Don't tell me you've been bulk buying them as presents for all your female relations?'

'Thus saving on time, effort and shoe leather? Isn't that what you advised?'

'Not quite.'

Somehow he had known that there would be precious few Brownie points for admitting to such a lack of imagination. The truth at least had the virtue of being surprising. 'No, well, actually, I bought that copy for myself.'

'Oh, sure,' she said. 'You're a new man through and through.'

Her scepticism was beginning to irritate him. 'The idea amuses you?'

'You don't really expect me to believe that you cook for yourself, Nick?'

'Men have to eat too, you know.'

'In my experience they usually manage that by getting some poor woman to cook for them.'

'Really?' Some of the women who had wanted to cook for him had been a long way from poor, but he didn't think she was referring to their fiscal status.

He wondered why she so despised domesticated women. Did she think they were letting the feminist side down? 'Maybe you should try a better class of man,' he advised.

'Is that an invitation?'

'An invitation?'

Without thinking he stood back to let her precede him through the door. She didn't appear to notice this lapse or, if she did, she let it go, but once she was in the corridor she stopped and turned to face him.

'An invitation to dinner, Nick. I've never met a man who could cook before. To be honest I'm still not sure that I believe you can — but I'm prepared to be convinced. I'm free on Thursday evening, if you've a space in your diary?'

Not by so much as the twitch of a muscle did Nick betray his surprise. Was that all it took to melt the ice-lady? A little home cooking? Or was it simply that she couldn't resist the opportunity to catch him out in a lie? Did she think he'd wriggle and squirm to get out of it?

'Well, there's an evening track meeting at Crystal Palace that I'm supposed to attend. We're sponsoring one of the events.' He waited while her face arranged itself into the superior kind of smile that suggested she had expected some feeble excuse. Then he shrugged and grinned. 'But I don't imagine I'll have any trouble finding someone to go in my place. Shall I pick you up at around eight?'

It was her turn to be surprised, but if she was she didn't let it show either. 'Won't you be occupied with your sauces?' she asked, making a little stirring gesture.

Frankly, he hadn't a clue. He had no idea what making a sauce entailed, but he knew it couldn't be difficult — his mother could do it for heaven's sake.

'I won't know until I've decided what to cook. Perhaps I'd better send a car for you.'

Her enigmatic look faltered slightly as she realised that he was serious. Then she lifted one elegantly clad shoulder a fraction of an inch. 'At eight? Why not? What have I got to lose?'

'Your waistline?' he suggested, recalling Cassie's comments about calories.

She gave him a disbelieving look before returning his book and heading for the meeting, one hundred-per cent businesswoman again, her entire being focused on the launch of a new line in ladies' golfing equipment.

Yet once when he looked up from the projected sales figures he was quoting to the team he caught her looking at him, her forehead creased in a slightly puzzled frown, and it was all he could do to stop himself from smiling.

Every woman had a weak spot. Even if it was only the desire to see a man make a fool of himself. He wondered about Cassie Cornwell and what her weak spot was. Not that kind of cynicism, he was prepared to bet any amount of money. She had the kind of eyes that would melt at a litter of puppies. Or the sight of snow falling on

Christmas morning. Or a new baby grasping at her finger . . .

'Nick?'

He started at the sound of his name and glanced up to discover half a dozen pairs of eyes looking up at him expectantly. It took a moment to clear the appealing image of Cassie Cornwell and puppies and Christmas in front of a log fire from his brain. What did it was the distinctly predatory look he surprised in Veronica Grant's eyes.

It was a momentary expression, almost instantly replaced by the cool, slightly distant look she normally adopted. He might have imagined it. But it gave him the uncomfortable feeling that she wasn't in the least bit taken in by his 'new man' act. And that if she caught him out in a lie he'd never be allowed to forget it.

* * *

Cassie had been cooking since she was old enough to stand on a chair and knead a piece of dough at her mother's side and she always found the beating, the kneading, the careful combining of ingredients as she prepared a favourite recipe therapeutic.

But ever since she had turned down Nick Jefferson's invitation to lunch nothing, not even the creation of a new pasta dish, had been able to shake her of the conviction that she had made a mistake. And it infuriated her. She slammed down the dough on the work surface in her kitchen and proceeded to take her feelings out on it. Nick Jefferson was not her kind of man and never would be. In a hundred years. And she certainly wasn't his kind of woman.

His kind of woman was tall as a tree, with sucked-in cheeks and a bone structure that *showed*. The kind of woman who lived on carrot juice and a few leaves of lollo rosso. The kind of woman who wouldn't dare to take three boisterous boys on a visit to an ice-cream factory in case the calories somehow managed to seep in through her pores. Remembering the hard work she'd had to put in at the gym afterwards, she had to admit that it was a distinct possibility.

She'd certainly be a woman with more sense than to offer to take those same three boys camping . . .

And, as if that wasn't bad enough, her brother-in-law had ridiculed the campsite she had picked out . . . the one with civilised plumbing, hot showers, a swimming pool and a camp store as well as organised activities with trained counsellors . . .

'That's not camping, that's a holiday camp,' Matt had scoffed. And her heart had sunk like an undercooked sponge as she had listened to his rose-coloured memories of his own boyhood camping trips. He had waxed lyrical about how they had fished and canoed and swum naked as the sun came up. And Mike and Joe and little George had listened too. At least Joe and George had. She had seen their ecstatic little faces absorbing every last detail. Mike had been quieter. She was worried about Mike.

'You can't expect my sister to take the boys somewhere like that,' Lauren interjected irritably. 'We'll have to take them with us to Portugal.'

Matt had no trouble in equalling his wife's irritation. 'I thought the whole point of this holiday was to get away from the children . . . ' Mike got up and left the room. 'Mike!'

'Oh, let him go,' Lauren said. 'Having him around is like living with a permanent headache.'

Cassie glanced after the boy, wondering if he'd heard. But it was her sister who was worrying her most. She had a pinched look about her mouth and angry eyes. She was looking for an excuse for the kind of row that would leave her free to walk out. Cassie refused to give her that excuse.

'For heaven's sake, Lauren,' she said lightly, 'anyone would think I was a grade A wimp to listen to you. We'll have a lovely time, won't we, boys?'

Lauren gave her a look that suggested she was fooling herself.

Was she? She'd put on a brave face for Beth, and the camp she'd chosen had sounded positively civilised. But to give Matt a chance to put things right she would willingly put up with a few days' discomfort.

'You're right, Matt,' she continued, with as much conviction as she could muster. 'Uncommercial sounds like much more fun. Book the site, mark the place on the map and we'll make like pioneers, won't we, boys?'

And pioneers was probably right. She was well aware that 'uncommercial' was shorthand for an absence of any kind of running water, and 'untouched' meant that the toilet facilities would involve the enthusiastic use of a shovel.

Then she gave herself a mental shaking. She had volunteered for this trip and it was a small enough sacrifice to make to save her sister's marriage. Although she rather thought she'd pass on swimming naked in some freezing

Welsh lake at dawn.

She put the bread dough in a greased bowl and covered it with a damp cloth while she waited for it to rise. Then she turned out a solid, cut-and-come-again fruit loaf she had been making for their trip. And after that she started to make a shopping list. A long shopping list.

If she was going pioneering, she had better be prepared for any eventuality.

★ ★ ★

Nick had always managed to eat very well without ever developing his culinary skills beyond the ability to make a decent cup of coffee. If pushed, he could make a slice of toast, even a sandwich. But he'd always considered the kitchen very much a female province and women, in his experience, couldn't wait to get in there and display their home-making skills, presumably in the hope they would become a permanent fixture. He'd never discouraged them. He'd never made any promises either.

He enjoyed home cooking as much as the next man, but not to the point that he was prepared to give up his independence for it.

But now all that was about to change. He sat at his desk and opened Cassie's book. It was organised neatly into courses and as he slowly turned the pages he could almost see her in some big, comfortable kitchen, full of the scent of herbs and baking bread, surrounded by earthy vegetables fresh from the garden.

Romantic nonsense, of course. She was a professional cook and almost certainly worked in a stainless-steel kitchen that had all the atmosphere of a hospital operating room.

He bypassed the recipes for rich vegetable soups. Somehow he didn't think that Veronica was the kind of woman to eat 'hearty'. No. He'd start with something simple. Something cold that could be prepared in advance and left in the fridge. His sister did it all the time.

Oysters? He grinned. No. That would be too obvious. And he prided himself on not being obvious. Smoked salmon would be better. With that special dill mayonnaise Helen made. And thinly sliced home-made bread. She'd part with a loaf if he asked her for one. Elegant, but easy. Pleased with himself, he made a note on the pad beside him. Round one and so far he hadn't done a thing.

What next? Something unusual, something that would convince her that he hadn't picked it up from a cook-chill cabinet at the supermarket. He would have liked to call Cassie and ask her advice. But he didn't have her number. Beth would know it, of course. But Beth would be too interested in why he wanted it. And jump to all the wrong conclusions. Instead he called his sister.

'Helen, how are you?'

'Busy. What do you want?' she asked suspiciously.

'Is that any way to speak to your big brother?'

'Nick, darling, I'm not one of your doting fillies, so please don't use your butter-wouldn't-melt-in-my-mouth voice with me; I know you too well to be taken in. What do you want?'

He considered acting hurt. But she was his sister. And, as she said, she knew him too well to be fooled. 'Advice. I'm cooking a meal for someone tomorrow night — ' She began laughing before he could finish. 'What's so funny?' he demanded.

'Oh, come on, Nick. Surely you don't have to ask? You couldn't boil water without burning it.' Then, before he could reply, she said, 'Oh, I get it. You want me to cook the meal for you and hide in the pantry between courses. Sorry, sweetheart,' she continued, before he could deny it, 'I'm giving a dinner for Graham's boss tomorrow night and his promotion rests on the piquancy of my chicken chasseur and the lightness of my pastry. Call a caterer. Or better still take the girl somewhere romantic. That usually does the trick — '

'Helen!'

'Doesn't it?'

'Not on this occasion.' Nick gritted his teeth. 'She thinks I can cook.'

'Where on earth would she get an idea like that about you?' Helen asked, hooting with laughter. Why did women always *laugh*? 'You didn't lie to the poor woman, did you?' Nick was interested to note that Helen referred to Veronica as a 'poor woman', too. Maybe they should meet and compare notes.

'No, I didn't. She found a cookery book on my desk and sort of jumped to conclusions.'

'A cookery book? What on earth ... oops ... was it my birthday present?'

'More or less,' he hedged.

'Even so. Is she soft in the head?'

'Does she have to be? Cooking can't be *that* difficult. Women do it every day of the week.'

'I guess it must be all that practice that makes us perfect,' she agreed, with suspicious sweetness. 'Let me know

71

how it turns out, Nick. Better still, take pictures; I can always use a really good laugh.' And she hung up.

'Helen!' Then, 'Damn!' He hadn't even had the chance to ask her for the bread and mayonnaise.

He considered calling his mother. But not for more than ten seconds. He'd had a basinful of being laughed at.

He'd make his own mayonnaise. He'd do it all. He'd got a cookery book. He could read. If Helen could cook chicken chasseur, so could he. He looked through Cassie's book. It wasn't there. He was beginning to understand why there was such a big market in cookery books.

* * *

He stopped at the supermarket on his way home. It wasn't something he did very often — he had a lady who came in every day to clean and organise the essentials of life, although she'd made it plain from the start that she didn't cook. Even if she had he wouldn't have asked her. He had something to prove to all those scoffing women.

Tonight he would have a practice run. Tomorrow — well, tomorrow his chicken with grapes, lemon and soured cream would make Miss Veronica Grant eat her words.

He manfully grasped a trolley with one hand and with his shopping list in the other he set about finding all the ingredients he would need. He had paused between a pyramid of canned peaches on special offer and a stack of cornflakes that would have given the Jefferson Tower a run for its money, wondering where to find the dried herbs, when he spotted Cassie Cornwell pushing an overloaded trolley that seemed to have a mind of its own.

She was too distracted by the task of preventing the shopping cart from knocking down the tower of cornflakes to notice him. The urge to let them tumble was, for just a moment, wickedly tempting. But then he realised that this was a God-given opportunity to pick her brains so he took pity on her and, taking hold of the front of the cart, pulled it straight.

Cassie looked up, a smile of thanks already on her lips, but as their eyes connected over a bumper-sized pack of breakfast cereals she blushed. 'Oh, it's you.'

'It was the last time I looked in a mirror,' he agreed. The blush was oddly gratifying; her lack of enthusiasm at encountering him was not. 'I take it this mound of food is for your camping trip? Or are you an impulse shopper?' he enquired.

Cassie had an impulse to throw something at the man. For appearing suddenly like that, before she could warn her body not to do anything stupid. She just knew she was blushing like an iced fancy that had been mugged by the cochineal.

'No.' He picked up the box of frosted cereals and turned it over. 'No.

Somehow I don't see you eating these for breakfast.' Cassie wondered what he did see her eating, but she managed to restrain herself from enquiring. He told her anyway. 'A girl like you understands that breakfast is the most important meal of the day. I see you tucking into something wholesome and filling. Soft creamy scrambled eggs with crisp bacon, toast, home-made marmalade and Jamaica Blue Mountain coffee?' he suggested.

Did that mean he thought she was fat? 'All that cholesterol and caffeine. What's healthy about that? I start the day with plain organic yogurt, fresh fruit and Earl Grey tea. No milk,' she replied crisply. Let him pick the bones out of that.

'Not even at the weekend?' He sounded disappointed and she had a sudden suspicion that he'd just betrayed his own breakfast favourites.

'Not even at Christmas.' She glanced in his cart. Expensive ready-skinned chicken breasts, two cartons of soured cream, lemons, grapes and a packet of rather sad-looking dill weed. 'What's a good-looking bachelor like you doing in a place like this, Nick? I should have thought your willowy blonde would be the one dashing around worrying about dinner.'

'You shouldn't listen to everything Beth tells you. Besides, I told you I was going to try out one of your recipes.'

'The chicken with grapes?' He nodded. 'You've got an awful lot there. Are you inviting all the neighbours in to share your triumph over the cooker?'

'Actually I'm having a dummy run before I try it out on . . . anyone else.'

He was cooking for the blonde? A tall, willowy, hollow-cheeked blonde? He *must* be smitten. The idea would have been oddly touching, if she hadn't been sure it was just a stunt to impress the girl. If she hadn't felt just a little envious that he would go to so much trouble to get her into bed. 'Well, watch the sauce doesn't curdle,' she advised. Then she frowned. 'What's the dill for?

76

It should be rosemary.'

'A mustard and dill mayonnaise. I thought I'd start with smoked salmon.'

'That's safe,' she agreed. She didn't make it sound like a compliment.

'Safe?'

'You just take it out of the packet and put it on the plate. There's nothing to burn.'

'There's the mayonnaise to make,' he pointed out.

'Buy a good one, add a dollop of that soured cream, a spoonful of whole-grain mustard and some freshly chopped dill. She'll never know the difference.'

'Is that what you do?'

'No, but then I'm a professional cook. And in my professional opinion you shouldn't use these.' She picked up the packet of herbs lying in the bottom of his cart. 'They're well past their best.'

'They were all that was available. And there was no fresh rosemary. I was looking for the dried herbs.'

She tutted condescendingly. 'You're breaking the first rule of cooking, Nick.

Never use second-rate ingredients. And if you can't find what you need in the supermarket cook something else.' She caught the fleeting look of panic that crossed his face and laughed. 'Don't worry, I've got fresh herbs in my garden . . . ' Now why on earth had she said that? Well, it was too late to back out of her rash offer. 'You're welcome to some. If you like.' And she was blushing again, which was totally ridiculous. She turned quickly away and grabbed a can of special offer peaches that she didn't want.

'That's very kind of you, Cassie.'

Stupid more like. 'Well, you did buy two copies of my book. Was your sister pleased with her present?'

'She hasn't seen it yet. It isn't her birthday until the weekend.'

'Maybe you should have her over for a birthday dinner and give her a demonstration.'

'I don't think so . . . I don't plan on making a career of this. Besides, she'll be in Paris.'

'Lucky woman,' she said, with feeling. 'I'll be out on the trail of the lonesome pine.'

'*Where?*'

She laughed and shook her head. 'I'm exaggerating. I'm sure Morgan's Landing will be lovely.'

'Morgan's Landing? Oh, I see, your camping trip. Look, if there's any way I can help — with equipment or anything ... ' he added, quickly qualifying his over-hasty offer. Then rather wished he hadn't. Which was ridiculous.

'Equipment isn't a problem, Nick. My brother-in-law has everything we're likely to need.' Most of it relics from his own camping days. Heavy, old-fashioned, durable, weighing a ton — but she didn't want Nick thinking she was trying to get him involved with her trip. In any way.

'Oh, right.' Nick had the uncomfortable feeling that she had seen right through him.

'If you've finished your shopping

perhaps we should get out of here,' Cassie said. She abandoned the limp dill-weed on the cornflake mountain. 'If you can wait while I see this load through the check-out and follow me home, I'll get you those fresh herbs.'

Nick had a niggling feeling at the back of his neck that it would be more sensible to grab the pack she had abandoned on the cornflake stack and make do. But that would be settling for second best and he had never, in his entire life, settled for second anything.

4

Nick didn't know quite what he had expected — a small neat apartment in one of the new blocks overlooking the river, perhaps. They were the kind of places successful businesswomen seemed to be buying. And he supposed she must be successful. With a television series under her belt. And he knew that cookery books regularly topped the best-seller lists.

But she was obviously a great deal more successful than he had anticipated if her home was anything to go by. Not that it was large. But it was lovely. One of those narrow town houses built around the Cathedral close about three hundred years ago. They rarely came on the market and when they did they were snapped up.

The brick was aged and mellow, the door gleaming with fresh black paint and polished brass door furniture, and there were tubs of bright sunshine-yellow pansies on either side of the top step.

'This is nice,' he said as she ran up the steps to the door.

'I like it.' She unlocked the door, propped it open and turned back to unload her shopping.

'Big for one, though.'

'I need a lot of space.'

He had been probing and he was pleased with her answer, the 'I' rather than a 'we'. 'Have you lived here long?'

'It was my family home. My father was a clergyman. A canon. At the cathedral. It's been rented out for the last few years.'

'I remember Beth said you'd been away.'

'Yes, I've been living in London. It's where the work is, in catering.' She wasn't quite meeting his eyes, he noticed. So there was some other reason. A man?

'And television?' he suggested.

'And television,' she agreed.

'So why have you come back?'

Because some things had to be faced, lived with. Because it was either that, or sell the house she loved and allow Jonathan to take even this away from her.

'Because I don't do catering any more,' Cassie said. 'And television just means a few weeks filming for a series. I don't need to stay in London for that.'

'And this is home.' Nick looked around the elegant hall with its pale yellow walls and white mouldings. 'I can see why you'd hurry back the first moment you could.' But she wasn't listening, more intent on collecting her groceries from the car. 'Leave those,' he said, following her back down the steps. 'I'll bring your bags inside.'

Cassie had used the retrieval of her shopping to cut short a dangerous conversation. She turned, about to tell Nick that she wasn't some feeble bimbo who needed a man to carry her shopping, then changed her mind. It would sound so ungrateful, after all. And he was hardly to blame for Jonathan's shortcomings as a husband. As a man.

'Thank you,' she said, handing over her car keys. 'The kitchen's down in the basement.'

It took two trips to empty her car and Nick left the bags inside the hall before going back to lock it. The sleek white Italian sports car had been as much a surprise as her home. If he had thought about it, he would have expected something roomy to transport food and equipment.

And yet the car did match the unexpected spark of passion that had lit up the back of Cassie's golden brown eyes when he'd kissed her. It was something she went out of her way to hide beneath that lively tongue, but it was there.

'Something smells good,' he said as he ducked his head below a beam and looked with satisfaction around the basement kitchen. It was nothing like a hospital operating room, in fact it lived up to all his best fantasies. It was a room to be lived in and worked in. A place where friends and family could gather and eat informally.

A built-in dresser taking up one wall was lined with plates and dishes in all shapes and sizes that must have taken years to accumulate. There was an Aga and a large modern built-in oven and two hobs. And the stone-flagged floor was softened with woven grass matting.

In a roomy alcove, emphasising that this was the domain of a professional cook, there was a small desk on which there stood, amidst a clutter of papers and note-books, a very workmanlike computer, along with the same combined telephone answering machine and fax that he had in his own home. He automatically logged the number in his memory.

In contrast, against the wall was the oldest, squashiest sofa he had ever seen. It was occupied by an equally squashy-looking ginger cat whose vast golden curves spilled over the velvet cushion on which he was sleeping. As if sensing Nick's presence the cat opened one eye and glared balefully at him, daring him to do anything as condescending as tickle his ear.

'I've been experimenting with a new recipe.' Cassie, unloading chilled food into the fridge, turned in time to witness her cat's silent snub. 'Don't mind Dem, he's not very keen on men,' she said, apologising for her unsociable feline. Nick would have liked to ask why, but some instinct warned him that it would be tactless. 'Just dump all those bags on the table, Nick; I'll sort them out later.'

'Right.' He tried to identify the appetising mixture of scents. There was the unmistakably yeasty aroma of newly baked bread. And cakes. She'd been baking cakes. The smell sent him straight back to his mother's kitchen and the childhood pleasure of scooping the last of the mixture from the bowl.

But there was more. The earthier

scents of herbs and tomatoes mingled with the faintest suggestion of garlic that had been gently simmering to perfection. It was the kind of smell, Nick thought as he went back upstairs to the hall to collect the remainder of the bags, that filled a man with dangerous longings to be invited to stay for supper.

'Have you got time for coffee?' she asked. 'Or do you want to cut and run?'

Obviously supper was not on offer. 'Cut and run?' he repeated.

Cassie waved towards a pair of French doors that opened out onto a walled courtyard crowded with pots of herbs and brightly coloured flowers before turning away to fill the kettle. 'The scissors are on the hook by the door. Help yourself.'

'Oh, right.' He unhooked the scissors. 'Er . . . what does rosemary look like?'

'It's the grey spiky . . . ' Then she glanced at him, uncertain whether he was teasing.

'It might be safer if I make the coffee

while you cut the herbs,' he suggested, a smile etching deep lines into his cheeks.

'Safe' was not a word Cassie would have used in conjunction with Nick Jefferson under any circumstances. However, in this instance he was probably right and she wasn't prepared to have her precious herbs massacred by some ignorant novice. 'You'll find the coffee in the fridge,' she said, surrendering the kettle and waving in the general direction of the huge double-doored monster in the corner.

Nick plugged in the kettle and turned to the fridge. Opening a door, he found himself confronted by a bowl of chunky vegetables bathed in the tomato and herb sauce that had filled the air with such a delicious, stomach-wrenching aroma. Her experiment. He wondered if she had any vacancies for guinea pigs.

He found the coffee beans and looked around for a grinder. It was an old wooden machine, worked by hand, that went perfectly with the kitchen. It took a lot longer than his electric job, but he found the slow turning of the handle and the sharp, satisfying build-up of the scent of fresh coffee a whole lot more satisfying than pressing a button.

He spooned the resulting ground coffee into a cafetière and then looked round for sugar, opening an array of tall cupboards. He didn't find the sugar, but since the cupboards were half empty he thought he might as well repay Cassie for the herbs by putting the groceries away.

'That's terribly kind of you, Nick.' He turned to see Cassie watching him from the doorway, a spray of herbs held lightly in her slender little hands. But there was something about the way she was looking at him that suggested he'd just made a rather stupid mistake.

'I thought I'd help. While I was waiting.'

'Did you? Well, in future I suggest you stick to making the coffee and leave the thinking to me.'

He frowned, not sure what he'd done to annoy her. He'd only been trying to help. 'Why? Do you usually keep your groceries on the kitchen table?'

'No, I keep them where I can reach them. And unless you plan on sticking around to hand me down anything I happen to need . . . ' She left him to draw his own conclusions.

'You mean you left the top shelf bare on purpose?' She didn't bother to reply, since the answer was obvious. To anyone with half a brain. 'Because you can't reach it?' He was grinning broadly now, not in the least apologetic.

'Those cupboards are ridiculously high,' Cassie protested.

'Too high for you,' he conceded.

'Well, life would be desperately boring if we were all built like telegraph poles,' she said. '*Blonde* telegraph poles,' she added, unwisely.

'Desperately,' he agreed, unforgivably amused.

Blushing furiously, she turned away to take two mugs down from their hooks and as the kettle began to boil she reached for it. Nick beat her to it.

'I'm making the coffee,' he reminded her. 'I may be thick, but I do know how to make coffee.'

'One should be good at something.' And she glared at him, daring him to top that. For a moment their eyes locked, then from somewhere deep inside Cassie felt a desperate urge to giggle. She had to resist it, she simply had to . . . 'The trouble with you, Nick Jefferson, is that you're good at too damned much,' she added.

'Is that right?' He cocked an impudent brow. 'Would you care to elaborate?'

'No.'

'But it wasn't a compliment?'

'No.'

'Somehow I didn't think it was.' She hadn't forgiven him for kissing her. Or forgiven herself for enjoying the experience. And she *had* enjoyed it. He wondered what she would do if he kissed her again. If he just put his arm around that small waist, pulled her into his arms and simply kissed her. Would that damped-down passion bubble to the surface? Would she kiss him back?

He was seriously tempted to find out, because standing there, unencumbered with shopping, he could see that while her figure had a distinctly luscious quality her waist was invitingly small. She was a classic pocket Venus. And he had this sudden urge to pick her up and . . .

But a man could only take so many liberties and get away with it. He was sure that this time her response was likely to be swift and painful. No matter how much she enjoyed it a woman had to make a pretence at outrage. It was all part of the game. His favourite game. And he knew all the rules. So he resisted the urge to kiss her and instead pressed down the plunger on the cafetière before turning to the refrigerator and retrieving a carton of cream.

'Do you take yours straight, or with cream and sugar?'

Cassie loved cream in her coffee, but she had seen that speculative look in

Nick's eyes as they'd roamed over her figure. This was not a moment to indulge herself, it was a moment to display self-control, strength of character, an iron will ... before Nick Jefferson got entirely the wrong impression of her.

'Straight,' she said.

He poured the coffee and handed her one of the mugs. Then he tipped a great dollop of cream into his own. 'I couldn't find the sugar,' he said. Without a word she passed him a bowl that had been sitting on the counter-top almost in front of him. 'Oh. How could I have missed that?'

'I really can't imagine.' He added two heaped spoonfuls to his mug and then stirred it slowly. She was certain that he was doing it deliberately, as if he knew that she was already regretting her own self-denial. 'Do you work out?' she asked, leaning back against the table, eyeing his spare, suit-clad frame through the twin veils of lowered lashes and the fragrant steam rising from her coffee as she sipped at it.

'You think I should?'

'It's worth considering. If you always drink your coffee that way,' she added. 'And sitting at a desk all day . . . '

'Actually I run,' he said, before she could suggest he was in danger of running to fat. 'Every morning before I go into the office. You should try it.' His dark eyes swept over her own well-rounded figure. 'It's a hell of a lot more effective than black coffee.'

'God, but you're rude,' she gasped.

One corner of his mouth lifted it into a cock-eyed grin. 'It must be catching. I've never tried it before — refreshing, isn't it?' He apparently didn't expect an answer because he put down his mug and continued, 'Now, since I'm here I think it might be a good idea if I repaid the favour and checked out your tent. I'd hate to think of you lying in your lonely little sleeping bag while the rain drips through the canvas.'

Somehow she doubted that. 'I won't be lonely and I think you've done quite enough thinking for one day, Nick. I can handle a tent and you've got chicken to cook.' She put down her coffee and offered him the herbs in a quite unmistakable invitation to leave. 'And this is a residents-only parking area. If you stay any longer you'll be clamped.'

Despite her feisty, in-your-face attitude she was uncomfortable around him, Nick realised. That was why she wanted him to leave. And the way she snatched her hand back as he took the herbs and their fingers touched momentarily told him why. But not why she was fighting it so hard, which was much more interesting. After all, if she wasn't attracted to him it should be easy, shouldn't it?

Maybe he should have kissed her after all? Cheeks slightly flushed, her lips parted over small white teeth, she did look thoroughly kissable despite, or perhaps because of, her slightly defiant posture. But, as she'd reminded him, he had chicken to cook. And that was quite enough trouble for one day.

'Thanks for these,' he said. 'I'm sure they'll make all the difference.' He paused in the doorway and looked back. 'Oh, and do enjoy your trip,' he added civilly. 'I'll be thinking of you up to your knees in midges, mud and small boys.'

That was too much. 'I hope your sauce curdles,' she muttered through gritted teeth as she followed him up the stairs.

He must have heard her because he paused in the doorway and turned to face her with that grin firmly back in place. 'And I hope your tent falls down in the middle of the night. In the rain.'

'Ooooh!' Cassie felt like stamping. But she didn't. But only because she knew it would have made Nick Jefferson laugh.

He laughed anyway. It had suddenly occurred to him why he kept thinking about kissing Cassie Cornwell. It was because she had to look up at him. And when she did her mouth seemed to be offering an open invitation to do just that. And when someone kept offering such a tempting treat it seemed churlish to refuse.

But just as he bent to double-check her lips for the taste of strawberries she said, 'I warned you that you'd be clamped, Nick.' And as he spun around to check his car she banged the door shut on him.

For a minute she leaned back against it, her heart hammering like a drum as she waited for him to start banging on the big lion-headed knocker. But he didn't. Maybe he was just too pleased that she had been lying about the clamp to take offence at the way she had dodged his kiss. Or maybe he wasn't that bothered. With the blonde already lined up and waiting to be impressed why should he be?

Perhaps it was relief that brought a smile to her face at the thought of Nick Jefferson trying to impress a girl with his cooking. He would probably do it too, she thought, shaking her head. He was that kind of man.

Nick spun back as the door shut behind him and began to raise his fist to bang on the door. Common sense stopped him. That and the strange look he was getting from some woman who was chatting to a caller on her doorstep a few doors down. Not that he cared one jot what the old busybody might be thinking. But Cassie would undoubtedly hate to be the subject of doorstep gossip.

And he should be grateful to Cassie, not mad at her. She had seen the kiss coming and stepped back, stopping him from making a fool of himself. After all, didn't he have the very lovely Veronica Grant lined up and in his sights?

So what on earth was he doing even thinking about kissing Cassie Cornwell? It didn't make sense.

★ ★ ★

On the other side of the door, Cassie finally heard Nick's car pull away from the kerb and she let out her breath. Well, that was that. And a good thing too. Now she could be quite certain that he wouldn't come back. So that was all right. Wasn't it?

What on earth would the world come to if men got the idea that they could just go around kissing anyone they thought they might? Just because their lips looked as if they might taste like strawberries?

Did they?

Curious, she threw a swift glance at the elegant gilt-framed mirror hanging above a beautiful serpentine table. Then, furious with herself for being sucked into such vanity, she hurried back down to the kitchen. Glancing up at the cupboards he had filled for her, she grabbed a chair, climbed on it and began emptying them, determined to eradicate all signs of Nick Jefferson's presence from her kitchen and from her life.

★   ★   ★

Nick, wearing an old T-shirt and a pair of jeans that had seen better days, examined his ultra-modern kitchen with distaste. When he'd bought the cottage, he hadn't been interested in the kitchen and had left it entirely in the hands of his decorator.

She'd made a big point about making it a room where a man would feel at home. Apparently that meant black units, black marble countertops and a hell of a lot of stainless steel. The only colour was provided by a few dark red 'keynotes'. It was about as homely and inviting as the chilled food cabinet at the local supermarket.

Still, he had to admit that it was functional, equipped with every gadget available, all in stainless steel, of course, although he'd never had any reason to use them. Precious little reason to use the kitchen, come to that. It occurred to him that if the room had been just a little more inviting he might have spent more time in it.

But it was a workspace, not a place to

linger. There was nowhere to sit, unlike Cassie's kitchen with its comfortable old sofa, except for a couple of Bauhaus-inspired stools by the centre island.

He'd liked the way Cassie's kitchen had opened out onto the tiny courtyard garden, too. He bet she took her breakfast out there on sunny days. The idea was very appealing. Not that he lingered much over breakfast. Still, at the weekends, with someone like Cassie to chat to, it was a habit he could cultivate.

He looked around. Maybe he should have the whole thing torn out and redone. This time by a decorator chosen for her skill rather than her sex appeal.

The kitchen smelled all wrong, too, he decided, remembering the wonderful fusion of scents that had welcomed him into Cassie's kitchen. This one just smelled of the stuff his cleaner used to keep the surfaces gleaming, a sort of synthetic lemon smell that had about as much in common with citrus fruit as his kitchen had with home cooking. Well, that was all about to change.

He opened Cassie's book and consulted the recipe. First of all he needed a large frying-pan. That was all? He smiled with satisfaction. He knew how to handle a frying-pan.

They'd had a photo shoot when they'd produced the catalogue for the new camping equipment. Rather than hire models who wouldn't look as if they knew what they were doing, the entire family had got involved. They'd rented a field and camped for the weekend, inviting some of the sportsmen and women Jefferson Sports sponsored to join in the fun.

He was the one in front of the improved one-man tent, sitting on the tried-and-tested camp stool, prodding sausages being cooked over the latest in camping stoves in the frying-pan that was part of the new range of cooking utensils. They'd eaten them too, despite the fact that by the time he'd finished with them they had borne more resemblance to charcoal than meat. It had been freezing.

So, a frying-pan held no terrors for him. And the recipe was described as simple, something that looked pretty, but could be cooked in about thirty minutes. No problems, then.

He found a stack of stainless-steel frying-pans that looked as if they had never been used, chose the largest and sloshed in some oil and a dollop of butter and turned on the burner. How high? All the recipe said was, 'Heat the butter and oil in a large frying-pan.' He turned up the heat and then looked to see what he had to do next.

The dark red 'keynote' telephone rang and, still reading the book, he unhooked it from the wall.

'Nick Jefferson.'

'Nick, it's Graham. We've hit a snag over the Paris trip.'

'What kind of snag? Has Helen found out?'

'No, it's not a Helen snag. It's a grandmother snag. Your mother is too busy to look after the kids — ' he didn't add 'as usual' because they both knew that Lizzie Jefferson's charity work absorbed time the way a natural sponge soaked up water ' — and mine is going to Bournemouth for the week with some friends. She offered to cancel but — '

But she was the one who always had to find time for the grandchildren, while *his* mother spent her time on more deserving causes. 'No, she mustn't give up her trip. I'll talk to Mum. I'm sure if I explain she'll find a few days to give her daughter a birthday treat — charity begins at home after all — '

'But Nick, you don't understand — '

The smell of burning suddenly impinged on Nick's consciousness and he spun round to see the pan he'd left on the stove smoking hotly. He stared at it for a moment in disbelief before saying something short and extremely rude. 'Leave it with me, Graham,' he said, dropping the phone and Cassie's cookbook as he rushed to push the pan off the heat.

The pristine pan was now black and pungent with burnt oil. All at once the scent of synthetic lemons seemed very appealing.

Nick returned the telephone receiver to the cradle, picked up Cassie's book and switched on the extractor fan. He filled the sink with hot water and submerged the pan, leaving it for his cleaner to deal with when she came in in the morning. Then he took the next, slightly smaller pan from the stack and with grim determination began again.

This time he carefully watched the butter melt into the oil before slipping the chicken breasts into the hot fat. There was a satisfactory sizzling noise and the meat began to brown. What next? He turned back to consult the oracle.

'Add the finely grated rind of one lemon, plus the juice and 5 ml of chopped fresh rosemary.'

It took him a while to find a grater and as he began to rub the lemon over the finest cutters it occurred to him that it would have been advisable to have done this before he started to cook the chicken. Why on earth didn't the book suggest that?

He lifted the grater to check his progress. The amount of rind produced was practically invisible and the chicken was beginning to brown rapidly. He switched to a bigger cutter and the skin began to come off in much more satisfying chunks. He dumped it in the pan.

Juice. There was a squeezer somewhere, but he didn't have time to look for it. Instead, he grabbed the nearest knife and hacked the denuded lemon in half, then held it over the pan and squeezed it, hard. Several pips joined the juice but he didn't have time to worry about that either.

Chop the rosemary. How much was 5 ml? He banged the knife over a sprig of rosemary — should he have washed it first? — and flung the roughly chopped result in with the chicken. Okay. What else?

'Add 150 ml of good chicken stock.'

Chicken stock? Nick Jefferson regarded the items on his kitchen table. There was a carton of soured cream and a bunch of white grapes. No chicken stock. Good, bad or indifferent.

5

Cassie was standing on a chair washing out her cupboards when the telephone began to ring. Since she'd had to get up there to sort them out, it had seemed as good a moment as any to give them a good scrub. Cleaning cupboards had always been a good way of taking her mind off things she would really rather not think about.

There were, she realised, quite a few things she would rather not be thinking about right now. Nick Jefferson was one of them. Jonathan was another. The trouble was that ever since her encounter with Nick Jefferson, Jonathan had been pushing himself to the forefront of her mind.

It wasn't really surprising. He hadn't looked like Nick, but he had had the same warm smile, the same flirtatious charm. And he had been quite as impossible to resist.

At twenty-two, with no one to please but herself, she hadn't seen any need to resist. She had fallen head over heels in love. It was what life was about. You grew up, you fell in love, you married and lived happily ever after. At least that was the way it was supposed to happen. In her case the 'happily ever after' part had been painfully brief.

Cassie didn't bother to climb down from the chair and answer the phone, but continued wiping the shelf with total concentration, leaving the answering machine to deal with her caller.

The ringing stopped as the machine cut in. She heard her own voice explaining that she was unable to come to the phone right now, asking the caller to leave a message after the tone. Then there was the long beep of the tone.

'What the hell is chicken stock, Cassie?' Cassie jumped as Nick Jefferson's angry voice rang out across the kitchen, knocking against the bowl of soapy water so that it slopped over the edge and onto the floor. 'I'm halfway through this damned recipe and suddenly you throw chicken stock at me . . . ' Cassie would have liked to throw a lot more. 'No, no, wait, not chicken stock. *Good* chicken stock. Tell me,' he asked nastily, 'do people ever deliberately use a bad one?'

'It doesn't mean — ' She stopped. Talking to an answering machine was scarcely a sign of an ordered mind.

'And why don't you warn people to do all the fiddly bits first?' he added.

'Because anyone with half a brain would know that,' she replied. Then she frowned. Wouldn't they? Her books were written for experienced cooks, but still . . . maybe she *should* make stuff like that clearer. Or write a special book for beginners; not everyone learned to cook at their mother's knee.

There was a long moment of silence from the answering machine, presumably while he waited for her to pick up the receiver obediently and answer him. Cassie ignored it, deep in thought as she considered what a simple, learn-as-you-go cookery book would entail, how her television company would feel about running a series on basic cookery . . .

'Damn it, I know you're there, Cassie, so you'd better pick up the phone and answer me, or I'll write to that woman on the television and expose you and your cookery books as frauds . . . '

'Drat the man,' she muttered irritably. How long was he going to go on complaining? He'd use up the entire tape at this rate. Why didn't he phone his sister and ask *her* how to make a stock? And how had he got her number anyway? It wasn't listed. Had he memorised it from the phone when he was looking around her kitchen? Or had Beth, still fantasising about being her matchmaking fairy godmother, given it to him? Well, it didn't matter.

Just because he'd bought a copy of her book, or even two copies, and just because he'd kissed her — at least that had only been once — he didn't have the right to call her up whenever he felt like it, especially when all he wanted from her was help to impress some blonde bimbo with his phoney cooking skills. And he had the nerve to accuse her of being a fraud!

It was definitely time she put Nick Jefferson right about one or two things and now was as good a time as any.

She spun round, planning to jump down and give him a piece of her mind, but the chair, unsteady on the old stone-flagged floor, wobbled as she moved, throwing her off balance. And as she lurched forward in an attempt to save herself it went away from her, falling backwards.

Cassie let out a yell that sent Dem nervously scooting beneath the sofa and grabbed for the cupboard door with both hands.

For a moment she hung there as waves of relief at her narrow escape swept over her. Then the old hinges, deciding they had had quite enough of that kind of treatment, thank you very much, parted company with the wood and Cassie was deposited without ceremony in an untidy heap on the floor.

★ ★ ★

Nick hung on, certain that Cassie was home. He'd left her less than an hour before and she hadn't looked in any hurry to get somewhere. Just get rid of him. Which was hardly surprising. She seemed to bring out the worst in him. And yelling at her down the phone was not the way to win her sympathy, or her help. He dragged his fingers through his hair and took a deep breath.

'Cassie . . . look, I'm sorry . . . I shouldn't have shouted but you've no idea of the mess I'm in here . . . Please pick up the telephone and talk to me. I'm desperate.'

Nothing. Well, what did he expect? Yelling at her like that had hardly been out of the *How to Win Friends and*

Influence People manual. In fact it hadn't been like him at all; he couldn't think what had come over him. He'd send some flowers by way of apology and then . . .

And then he'd forget it. Cassie Cornwell was absorbing altogether too much of his time. He lifted one of his shoulders in the smallest of shrugs and was just about to hang up when he heard something. Something that sounded remarkably like the receiver at the other end crashing to the stone floor of her kitchen.

'Cassie?'

'Buy a packet of stock cubes, Nick, and follow the instructions . . . ' Her voice was tight, as if talking was an enormous effort, and when she stopped there was a little catch . . . Was there someone with her? A man? Was that why she had been so eager to get rid of him? She'd been expecting someone?

Something in his gut tightened at the thought of a man holding her, kissing her, perhaps undressing her right now.

It made him feel . . . helpless, a little desperate, even angry. He knew he should just hang up, but he couldn't. 'That's not what *you'd* do, though?' he persisted, his ears straining for some clue.

'Nick, believe me, you don't want to know how to make a stock from scratch.'

'It's difficult?'

'No, but . . . Trust me. Take the short cut. Everybody does.'

'I'm not everybody.'

'Ain't that the truth. Go away, Nick, please; I can't handle this right now.' That didn't sound much like a girl in the throes of sexual excitement. It sounded . . .

'Cassie? Is something wrong?'

Cassie laughed. Sort of. She'd fallen beside her desk and was sitting on her kitchen floor propped against the wall, her ankle screaming in agony where she had twisted it beneath her, while some man demanded a cookery master class over the telephone. No, not just some man, she corrected herself. Mr Nick slay-'em-in-the-aisles Jefferson.

Well, he wasn't slaying her, in the aisles or anywhere else. Not if she could help it. Certainly not right now.

'Wrong, Nick? What could possibly be . . . ?' Cassie attempted to bite back a yell as Dem emerged from beneath the sofa and rubbed anxiously against her foot; she didn't entirely succeed. 'Wrong?' came out as a long, strangulated cry.

The tiny hairs on Nick's neck rose as he realised that it wasn't passion that was causing her to catch her breath, but pain. He didn't bother to ask what was wrong again. 'Hold on, Cassie,' he said. 'I'll be right there.'

'No! There's no need — ' But it was too late. He had already hung up.

Cassie allowed herself the luxury of a small groan. She'd pulled the phone down from its cradle because, having nearly killed herself in her attempt to answer it, it had seemed rather stupid not to bother simply because she was in agony.

Now she let it drop on the floor beside her while she mentally gathered herself for the crawl across the kitchen to the first-aid box containing witch hazel and a crêpe bandage. Dem crept up beside her and began to tread anxiously against her thigh, little needle claws digging in as he butted his head against her hand.

She hauled the cat onto her stomach and fondled his ears. She'd make the effort to move soon, she promised herself, but another few minutes wouldn't hurt.

She wasn't worried about the imminent arrival of Nick Jefferson. He couldn't get in unless she climbed the stairs to the front door and opened it for him. And since there was no way she could do that he would just have to go away again.

And a very good thing, too, she told herself. Men like Nick Jefferson were nothing but trouble. At twenty-two she hadn't known that. At twenty-seven she didn't have the same excuse.

* * *

Nick stopped only to turn off the hob, eyeing the two dried-up, overcooked chicken breasts with resignation. They didn't look remotely edible. They certainly bore no resemblance to the photograph in Cassie's book. Maybe his sister was right. Maybe it would be a good idea to confess all to Veronica and take her out somewhere unbelievably expensive for a meal.

She might even be flattered that he had gone to so much trouble in an attempt to impress her, especially if he turned the whole thing into a joke against himself. Beneath that reserved, oh-so-cool exterior, Miss Veronica Grant must have a sense of humour, surely?

The only danger with such a plan was that Veronica might find the situation so funny that she would be compelled to share the joke with Lucy, her secretary . . . knowing full well that five minutes after that the entire staff of Jefferson Sports would be having a

118

good laugh at his expense. He scraped his fingers back through his hair once more. How on earth had he ever got himself into this mess?

It scarcely mattered. But he wasn't about to be defeated by a piece of chicken. Before he beat the chicken into submission, however, he had to go and find out what had happened to Cassie, find out what had made her cry out like that. No matter how loudly she'd shouted, 'No!' down the telephone.

It was a little less than ten minutes before he'd tucked the black wedge of his Porsche behind her sleek little Alfa. It was only then that he thought about how he'd get in. If she was down in the basement, hurt, she wouldn't be able to get to the door.

He knocked and waited impatiently, leaning over the iron balustrade to peer down into the basement area, hoping to be able to see into the kitchen, but the window was high and narrow and the angle was all wrong. He retreated to the pavement, but even bending right down he still couldn't see more than a few feet. But she hadn't come to the door, so she must be down there. Hurting. The word squeezed at his gut. He had to do something.

He glanced up and down the street. There must be some way into the courtyard at the back. He hadn't noticed a gate, but then he hadn't actually gone beyond the French doors.

He walked to the end of the street, turned a corner. There was a door set into an eight-foot wall that linked with the street backing onto Cassie's house. It was locked, but it had to be the rear way in.

He jumped, grabbed the top of the wall and hauled himself up. As he suspected, behind the door was an alleyway running between the houses, each with a gate leading into a courtyard garden. Since it was quite possible that those gates were locked too he didn't bother to jump down into the alley and test his theory but walked quickly along the top of the wall.

Someone shouted at him, demanding to know what he was up to, but he took no notice as he counted the houses until he came to Cassie's. Not that he could have mistaken it. Her yard was filled with terracotta pots over-flowing with geraniums and nasturtiums and pansies, and as if that wasn't enough of a clue the evening was full of the unmistakable scents of thyme and rosemary.

* * *

Cassie hadn't, after all, bothered to move. She felt a touch light-headed and couldn't face the haul across the kitchen floor. And Dem lying across her stomach seemed to weigh a ton. Totally immovable.

Anyway, the pain in her ankle was easing a little, so perhaps lying perfectly still was the sensible thing to do. The only problem was that she was seeing things. Or, at least, not things. People. A person. Nick Jefferson to be precise.

And he appeared to be walking on air.

She blinked and he disappeared. Oh, well. Maybe she had just been imagining it. She had been thinking about him riding to her rescue like some latter-day knight errant in that late twentieth century alternative to a trusty steed, a black sports car.

Which one would he be? Not Galahad, that was for sure. Galahad was the good guy, pure in body and heart; he would never have stolen a kiss. That was the trouble with good guys. They were predictable. Safe. And just a little bit dull.

No one could ever accuse Nick Jefferson of being dull. Which was presumably why she'd been wasting so much time thinking about him. It was so long since anyone had kissed her — not that they hadn't wanted to but after Jonathan she'd been very careful not to get involved with relationships that involved kissing. The safe, predictable men didn't do anything for her. And the dangerous ones . . .

Of course Nick had stolen his kiss. And stolen kisses, no matter how sweet, didn't count. Did they? Not enough to excuse hallucinating about him, anyway.

She closed her eyes for a moment, just while she got her head straight. And when she opened them again there was a dark shadow in the doorway, a man's broad shoulders blocking out the deepening twilight. She let out a cry of alarm and Dem, using her stomach as a springboard, fled for cover once more.

'Cassie?'

'Nick?' She blinked as he reached for the light-switch and snapped it on, throwing up her hand as the light temporarily blinded her. Then she saw him clearly, discovered that she hadn't been hallucinating after all and questions began to crowd into her head. Like, what did he think he was doing, walking into her kitchen without so much as a by-your-leave? And how the devil had he got there when she was surrounded by an eight-foot wall? And why, when she was furious with him for giving her such a fright, was she feeling so deliriously glad to see him?

'What happened?' Nick demanded.

But he didn't need to ask. The toppled chair, the broken cupboard door told their own eloquent tale. She'd climbed up to retrieve the things he'd put away on the top shelf after he'd walked out without giving a thought to how she would get them down. Well, now he knew. By climbing on a rickety old chair, that was how. She had fallen and it was his fault.

As Nick moved out of the shadows Cassie could see that his face was creased with concern. Or maybe he was just frowning. He had sounded decidedly irritated on the phone. All that fuss over a drop of stock. What was it about men? They always had to make such a drama out of the simplest thing. Like this.

She'd fallen off a chair, that was all. She could handle it. But before she could tell him that he was crouched at her side, his fingers at her wrist, feeling for a pulse, and without warning she was overcome by an irresistible impulse to giggle.

'What's so funny?' he demanded.

'You are. I've twisted my ankle, Nick. You won't find that out by feeling my pulse.'

But he was still frowning. 'It seems a bit erratic to me.' He pushed the hair that had slipped from its comb back off her face, holding it there while he peered at her forehead. 'Did you hit your head? I'd better call an ambulance,' he said, without waiting for her reply.

She could have told him that the only reason her pulse was jumping about was that he was leaning over her, his jaw inches away from her cheek. If he turned and looked into her eyes, his mouth would be all lined up and ready to do what he'd been on the point of doing when she'd shut the door on him. Why had she stopped him? She'd wanted him to kiss her. She would be lying to herself if she denied it. It was bad enough when someone else lied to you, someone who said they loved you, but lying to yourself was just asking for trouble.

She'd stopped Nick from kissing her because she was scared. Scared of being hurt. Which was ridiculous. How could he hurt her? You had to love someone before they could hurt you and she had promised herself never to fall into the love trap again.

But up this close she could see the day-old stubble of his beard, knew exactly how it would feel against her skin, and there was a yearning deep within her to raise her hand, rub it over his cheek and feel the roughness against her palm. Just to say his name. Nick. She tried it in her head. But she didn't say it out loud.

If she did that he would look at her, really look at her and see all that longing betrayed in her eyes. A sprained ankle wouldn't be any defence against what would happen after that. And that would end up hurting her a whole lot more than any sprain.

'Don't be ridiculous,' she said, snatching her hand back before common sense took a holiday. 'I don't need an ambulance. All I need is a touch of witch hazel and some strapping on my ankle and I'll be fine — ' She caught her breath as he turned away and ran his fingers lightly over her foot, her ankle. And it wasn't because of the pain.

'At least it's not broken.'

'I could have told you that, but I'm grateful for the second opinion, Dr Kildare,' she muttered, through gritted teeth. 'Now, if you feel up to doing something practical instead of practising your bedside manner, you'll find the first-aid box under the sink. I'm sure there's a crêpe bandage in there.'

'Yes, ma'am. But shouldn't I be doing something interesting with cold compresses first?' He glanced back at her, the corner of his mouth lifted in that impossibly sexy way that did far worse things to her than falling off a chair.

'Should you?' she demanded, refusing to play along. 'Do you know what a compress is?'

Well, that wiped the grin right off his face. But that concerned little frown that creased the space between his brows hadn't gone. 'You don't think much of me, do you, Cassie?'

'I'm sure you're trying very hard to impress me, Nick. The trouble is I can't think why.'

'Neither can I. It's a worry, isn't it?' He stood up and crossed to the big American fridge-freezer, opened the freezer section and began pulling out the drawers.

'What are you doing?'

'Looking for this.' He hefted a small packet of frozen peas in his hand. 'I wasn't sure if a high-and-mighty famous cook like you would stoop to such stuff.'

'My nephews like them.' Oh, good grief, their trip . . . 'Ouch!' This, as he applied the frozen pack of vegetables to her ankle. Then she said, 'It seems you *do* know what a compress is.'

'I come from a family of sportsmen. And women. My mother was a particularly fine hurdler ... only my untimely arrival put a stop to her Olympic hopes ... but I learned all about the many uses for frozen peas at her knee.' When he looked up at her the lopsided grin was back in place and her pulse danced another ridiculous little jig. 'It was sprained at the time.' He sat back on his heels. 'Actually I think this would be a whole lot easier if you were on the sofa. Put your arms around my neck.'

'I can get there — '

He did it for her and the jig in her pulse intensified to a reel as she stopped arguing and clasped her hands behind his head. Maybe she should get him to check it out again. She rather liked the way his fingers felt against her wrist. Which was as good a reason as any for not encouraging him.

'You'll put your back out,' she warned as he slid his hands beneath her. 'Then what would we do?'

'Not very much,' he admitted. His face was so close that she could see the tiny black flecks in his irises, the black flecks that made his grey eyes seem so dark. But apparently he didn't take her warning seriously, because he scooped her up and placed her on the sofa with about as much trouble as if she were a feather pillow. 'Certainly not what I'd like to do to you.'

'What's that?' Cassie demanded, and then blushed hotly, but he didn't appear to notice as he turned to pick up the peas. He reapplied them, without much ceremony, to her injured ankle.

'Put you over my knee and spank you for climbing on a rickety old chair. Haven't you got a stepladder?' he demanded.

'I lent it to my next-door neighbour.'

'You should have asked for it back. Here, hold this in place while I find the first-aid box,' he said. 'Then I'll strap it for you.'

'I can't wait,' she said, sweat beading her upper lip as she determinedly ignored the pain. She didn't want him changing his mind and calling an ambulance after all. Change the subject. Think of something else. No, not *that*! 'How did you get in, Nick?'

'At great risk to life and limb,' he said, hunkering down to search through the cupboard beneath the sink so that his strong thighs bulged against the soft cloth of his jeans. The man was dangerous enough in the civilising garb of a well-tailored suit; in old jeans and a T-shirt that clung to his torso, he was a menace. He turned and lifted the corner of his mouth again in the most economic version of a smile she'd ever encountered. She bit her lip to stifle a groan. 'Over the back wall.'

Cassie decided that a groan was perfectly in order after all. 'You really shouldn't have done that.'

'There's no need to worry, I'm not as incompetent as you; I didn't hurt myself,' he said, with characteristic flippancy.

'It isn't you I'm worrying about,' she

declared, suddenly furious with him not for the insult but for his stupidity. Did he *never* think? 'Someone's bound to have seen you and the neighbourhood watch will be all of a dither.'

'Actually someone did shout at me,' he confessed.

'Then listen out for sirens; the police will be round any minute.' As if on cue, there was a sharp rap at the front door. 'There, what did I say?'

He put his hand to his ear. 'I didn't hear any sirens.'

She glared at him. 'You'd better go and reassure whoever it is that I'm not being strangled over a hotpot, Nick. Or they really will call the police.'

But it was too late for that. Someone had already called the police and a few moments later Nick and a constable returned to the kitchen.

'Cassie, darling, Constable Hicks tells me that one of your neighbours reported an illegal entry. I explained what happened, but naturally he wants to reassure himself that you're safe and that I'm not just some axe-murderer spinning him a line.'

Darling? *Darling?* What was the man playing at now? Well, she'd show him that he wasn't the only one who could play games. She turned to the policeman.

'Thank goodness you've come, Officer. This man is a complete stranger — he just climbed over my back wall and walked in.'

It was a mistake. She shouldn't have done it; she knew that the moment the words were out of her mouth. The young policeman clearly didn't know what to think and glanced uncertainly at Nick, who was leaning against the doorway, his face expressionless.

'I told you, Officer, Miss Cornwell fell off a chair. I'm sure she must have bumped her head but she's refusing to let me take her down to Casualty.' He didn't say it in so many words, but his tone suggested she wasn't quite right in the head. Okay, so she deserved it. But did he have to look so pious about it?

'Mr Jefferson told me that you'd had a fall, miss,' the policeman said, turning back to her and starting from a point that might help him to make sense of the situation. 'Did you, er, bump your head? Maybe you should take his advice and go down to the hospital for a check-up.'

Nick caught Cassie's eye and raised one brow by a millimetre, suggesting that she'd asked for that. Well, maybe she had. Maybe she *was* crazy. She certainly felt just a little light-headed. But she was quite sure it had nothing to do with falling on that part of her anatomy. Still, she shouldn't be making light of the situation. It was not a laughing matter.

The policeman certainly wasn't amused. He was staring at her ankle, fetchingly draped with a rapidly defrosting bag of peas, without so much as the suspicion of a smile.

6

'I did have a fall,' Cassie confirmed quickly, 'but I didn't hit my head. And Nick came to my rescue,' she added, with an ingratiating smile, prompting the young constable to share the joke.

The policeman declined with a slight frown. 'I thought you said you didn't know Mr Jefferson?'

That was the trouble with a joke that fell flat. Having to explain it was so very . . . embarrassing.

'I know and I'm sorry, Officer . . . ' Sorry she'd ever started this. Sorry she'd offered Nick some herbs. Just sorry. 'It was a joke. A very bad joke,' she added hurriedly as his frown deepened. 'It was all Nick's fault, you see . . . ' Oh, no. That sounded even worse. It was true, of course. Everything was Nick Jefferson's fault. But he *had* raced to her assistance when he'd realised she was in trouble. But only, she reminded herself firmly, so that he could learn the secrets of a good stock . . . 'Nick called me and I was trying to get to the phone when I fell and twisted my ankle. Nothing serious. In fact he was just about to strap it for me.'

'Really?' Only a policeman could invest a word with such a depth of meaning, she thought. 'You're quite sure that it doesn't need professional attention?'

'Oh, no, he's quite capable of dealing with it, Officer.' She might be anxious to get rid of him, but not if it meant a trip to Casualty. 'Sprains apparently run in his family.'

'Is that so?'

Shut up, you idiot, she told her mouth as another attempt at humour, admittedly a feeble one, sank without trace. 'They're sportsmen . . .' Although as far as she could work out Nick Jefferson's success seemed confined to indoor games. 'And women,' she added. 'Jefferson Sports, you know . . .'

'Yes. I know.' Of course he knew.

Everybody knew the Jefferson building. She'd just have to make certain that she avoided it in future. 'Well, I won't delay Mr Jefferson's first aid any longer than necessary. If I could just have a few details for the record.' He turned to Nick. 'I wonder if you would be kind enough to go out to the patrol car and inform my colleague that I'll be with him very soon?' Nick turned without a word and left the room. When he had gone the officer glanced at the chair still lying on its side and the sad ruins of the cupboard door, before turning back to Cassie. 'Are you quite happy for me to leave now, Miss Cornwell?'

'Don't you want my name, rank and serial number?' she asked flippantly. Then gave herself a mental slap on the wrist. Just tell the man what he wants to know and let him leave.

'Not unless you want to make a complaint.'

'Complaint? I thought I'd explained — '

'If you'd rather talk to a female officer, I can arrange that.'

Cassie knuckled her forehead, convinced that she must have missed an entire chunk of conversation. Maybe she *had* banged her head, after all. 'I'm sorry, Officer. I really don't follow — '

'Someone from the DVU, the domestic violence unit,' he explained.

'The *what*?' She felt the blood drain from her face, the sickening nausea as she realised what he was suggesting. That Nick might have hurt her. That this was some domestic quarrel . . . that he had broken in and hurt her. And now she was too frightened to say anything . . . 'Oh, no,' she groaned. How on earth could she have been so stupid? Then, because the policeman was still waiting, and because she had to convince him that Nick was totally innocent, she repeated herself. 'Oh, no, *really*. Nick didn't . . . I mean, *honestly*. Oh, this is just so embarrassing.' The young policeman remained impassive. 'I was just teasing him. I'm sorry, really sorry. I shouldn't have done it but he just . . . ' She wasn't going to explain how she'd felt when Nick had called her 'darling'. 'Really. I fell off the chair trying to get to the phone when Nick called. He realised I'd hurt myself and came rushing over. I was just teasing him a little . . . ' She could have offered the answering machine as evidence, but somehow she didn't think this young man would be very impressed by the way Nick had been shouting at her . . .

'Why did he come over the back wall?'

'I couldn't get to the door and he doesn't have a key. He's a friend, Constable, not a lover.' It was important to convince him of that. Friends didn't hit you. 'I'm not his type, you see.'

'No?' The policeman finally offered a smile. 'I can't think why. I'd have said you were on the wish list of any red-blooded male who's seen you on television.' Which was sweet considering that she had to be five or six years older than him. A lifetime when you were his age.

'Maybe he doesn't watch that much television. But he has been incredibly kind. Risking a climb along the wall just to check that I was all right. If it hadn't been for him I could have been lying on the floor until my cleaner arrived in the morning.'

'Well, if you're sure?' He remained doubtful. 'We can't help unless — '

'I know.'

'And you don't need to go to Casualty?'

'I don't need to go to Casualty,' she confirmed carefully. 'Thank you.' She watched with relief as he closed his notebook and slipped it into his pocket. 'And thank you for coming so quickly. I might really have needed your assistance. I should thank whoever called you, too.'

'It was one of your neighbours. A Mrs Duggan?'

'Oh, yes.' The one who'd borrowed her steps. It had a certain symmetry . . . 'It's good to know people care.'

'You seem to be particularly blessed

in that department, Miss Cornwell.'

'Yes, I do, don't I?' Finally convinced, the young policeman bade her goodnight and departed and Cassie was finally able to let out a huge sigh of relief and lean back against the cushion.

'That'll teach you to tease the law,' Nick said.

Cassie turned her head. He was leaning against the doorframe, thick forearms folded over his chest. 'It was your fault,' she told him. 'I'd never have done it if you hadn't called me 'darling'. What on earth made you do that?'

'It seemed like a good idea to foster the cosy illusion of togetherness. My mistake. He sent me away so that he could find out if I'd been beating you up, didn't he?' Her face was all the confirmation he needed. 'I thought so. Still, it was worth it . . . '

About to offer her deepest apologies for putting his good name at risk, she did a double take. 'Worth it?'

'Just to hear you say that I was being

incredibly kind. And with such ringing sincerity, too.'

'It nearly choked me. This accident was entirely your fault, you know.'

'Was it?' He walked across the room, picked up the chair and tucked it back under the table then stood the cupboard door against the wall. 'You don't feel just a little bit responsible . . . ? I'm sure standing on a wobbly chair is firmly discouraged in the cook's handbook of kitchen safety.'

'It's not wobbly.' He rocked it to prove his point. 'It's the floor that's wobbly. And I wouldn't have been standing on a chair if you hadn't decided so high-handedly to put my groceries on the top shelf. And even then it wouldn't have been a problem . . . I was doing fine until you started shouting at me about chicken stock.'

'A mistake for which I did apologise. I was having a bad time with a recipe at the time. One of your recipes.'

'It happens.'

'To you?'

'To everybody. Thankfully very few people telephone to abuse me personally. What was the problem?'

'The problem was that I didn't know what I was doing,' he admitted. 'Will you help me, Cassie?'

She couldn't believe the nerve of the man. 'Take her out to dinner, Nick. That way there's a chance that you'll both enjoy the experience.'

'I can't. This isn't about enjoyment.'

'No?'

He shook his head. 'It's about winning.' He sat on the edge of the sofa and lifted the bag of peas from her ankle. 'How is it?'

'Bearable,' she said, refusing to wince. 'Do you always have to win?'

'I'm a Jefferson. In my family you win or die in the attempt. You'll need to keep your weight off this for a day or two,' he said as he began to roll a crêpe bandage in a neat figure of eight around her foot and ankle. 'Getting up and down stairs might prove something of a problem.'

'The stairs are the least of my worries. I'm taking three lively boys camping the day after tomorrow.'

'That's out of the question. You'll have to postpone it.'

'I can't.' He glanced up, the slightest frown creasing his brow. She shrugged. 'I promised the boys.'

'Well, you can't go on your own; you'll never manage.'

'Mike'll help me,' she said, with more confidence than she felt. Mike hadn't been his usual sunny self when they'd been discussing the trip.

'Mike?'

'My oldest nephew.'

'How old is that? You won't be able to drive, you know.'

'I'm borrowing my brother-in-law's estate. It's an automatic,' she said quickly.

'Nice try, Cassie, but it's your right ankle you've sprained.'

'Have you eaten yet?' she asked, in a determined effort to change the subject.

'No. My dinner was ruined by an

incompetent chef. What about you?' She shook her head. 'Shall I order a take-away?'

'Don't be silly, I've got a fridge full of food — '

'And an ankle that won't bear your weight,' he pointed out.

'Oh, but if I tell you what to do — '

'I've already messed up one kitchen tonight. What'll it be? Chinese, Indian?' he offered as he picked up the telephone receiver from the floor. 'A pizza?' he added doubtfully.

'Anything,' she said, just a touch breathlessly. No one ever bought food for her, they always expected her to do the cooking, and she felt ridiculously pampered as Nick ordered Chinese at great length. 'There's a bottle of wine in the fridge,' she said, when he'd finished. 'I could do with a drink.'

'Is that a good idea? What about shock, concussion?'

'As I keep telling people — I didn't bang my head. Why won't they believe me?'

He gave a telling shrug. 'I can't think. Corkscrew?'

'In the top drawer.'

'Glasses?'

'The cupboard above the sink.'

'Why doesn't your cat like men?'

His question took her totally unawares and for a moment she did a very good impression of a goldfish, but as he turned for an answer she said, 'Just good taste, I imagine.'

'Isn't he one himself?'

'Not technically.'

'Ouch!'

'You've obviously never kept a tom cat,' she retorted, 'or you'd know they're impossible to live with.'

'So I've been told.'

Cassie gave a little gasp, then to cover her confusion she leaned over and tried to coax him from beneath the sofa. 'Come on, Dem. Nick won't hurt you.'

'Dem?'

'Demerara. Like the sugar.' And as the cat slunk out from his hiding place and jumped up on the sofa beside her his pale golden fur caught the light.

'Oh, I see. The colour. My sister had a Labrador once, called Honey — Oh, damn! I've just remembered some-thing . . . ' He handed her a glass of wine. 'Can I use your phone?'

'Help yourself.'

He punched in a number but all he got was an answering machine. Speaking to his mother, he decided, was as difficult as trying to get through to the Prime Minister, but at least the PM had a secretary. 'This is Nick. Graham told me that he spoke to you about having Helen's kids, Mum. Look, I know you're busy but — '

'Nick, darling,' his mother said, picking up the phone.

'Oh, good, you're there. I thought you might be away — '

'Another five minutes and I will be. I'm just leaving for a UN conference in Nairobi. I'm sorry to mess up your plans, Nick. Maybe you can organise it again when I've more time?'

'You've never got any time,' he

reminded her tetchily. 'And it's Helen's birthday *this* week.'

'I know. I bought her a signed copy of Cassandra Cornwell's new cookery book when I was in town the other day.'

'So did I.'

'Really? Oh, dear. What a shame. And I gave her mine today because I won't be here on the day. Still, you'll think of something else.'

'You didn't organise a break in Paris for her as well, did you?'

'Of course not. I gave her a cheque so that she can choose something for herself.'

'Great.'

'She seemed pleased. You should have done the same. It would have been so much simpler. For everyone.'

'I went to the trouble of organising her a proper birthday present,' he said, through gritted teeth.

'Yes, dear, so Graham told me. It was a lovely thought. What a pity you didn't think about the children before you booked it.'

'With two grandmothers on standby I didn't think it was necessary.'

'Grandmothers have lives too, Nick. If you feel so strongly about it why don't you take some time off and look after the girls yourself? You know how fond of you they are. Now, I must go; the taxi's at the door.' And with that advice she hung up.

'Problems?' Cassie enquired as he replaced the receiver.

'You could say that. Four of them. All female.'

'Ah! Nothing you can't handle, then.'

He pulled a face. 'It seems I'm about to find out. What would you do with four little girls for five days, Cassie?'

'How old are they?'

'Between five and eight. Cute as kittens and as much fun — '

'When you can hand them back to their mother and walk away?' That was one problem she could empathise with.

He shrugged. 'A trip to McDonald's is one thing. But five days . . . '

'Take them away somewhere.'

'And spend all my time explaining who they are and why they're alone with me to suspicious matrons?' He topped up their glasses and eased himself alongside her on the sofa, sliding his arm behind her shoulders to give himself more room. Dem glared at him indignantly. 'I suppose you think I'm being selfish? You *volunteered* to take your nephews on a camping trip . . . ' With her cheek pressed against the side of his chest and her thigh tight up against his Cassie was finding any kind of thinking difficult. She could feel his heart hammering against his ribs, hear it thumping against her ear.

'And as if that isn't bad enough my mother bought Helen a copy of your book, too.' He glanced down at her. 'Signed,' he said. As if it were somehow her fault.

'I signed a pile before I left the store — for those people who couldn't make it that morning.'

'But Beth knew I'd bought one for Helen.'

'I'm sure Beth wouldn't have sold your mother a book knowing that you'd already done that, Nick. At least not without mentioning it. Maybe your mother went into the shop while we were at lunch?'

He'd been turned down for lunch in favour of Beth Winslet? He supposed he should be glad that it wasn't another man, but he couldn't quite make up his mind whether it was better or worse. 'Maybe she did. It doesn't matter now, because she's already given it to Helen. I might as well dump the one I bought her in the bin.'

Cassie thought that this might have been more tactfully put, but she didn't say so. She was having too much pleasure seeing his well-ordered world falling apart. But she somehow managed to quell an almost irresistible urge to giggle. 'Oh, dear,' she said, with mock sympathy. 'And there's still your dinner date to get through. Poor Nick. You're having a tough week.'

'It hasn't been all bad.' He raised his

151

glass an inch or two. 'After all, I met you.'

No, that was really too much. 'Oh, p-lease. You don't have to pretend, Nick. All you want from me is the chance to dazzle your blonde with a fancy recipe. Well, I'll tell you now that where I'm concerned flirting won't get you past go.'

'Won't it?' For a moment his gaze held hers, his dark grey eyes thoughtful, as if measuring just how far flirting *would* get him. And she remembered him saying that winning was everything. It wouldn't do to challenge this man to a contest of wills; in her weakened state she wouldn't stand a chance. Who was she kidding? In any state he was more than a match for her. 'Why not?'

'I don't flirt.'

Not intentionally maybe, Nick thought. But she used her eyelashes the way a Regency heroine would have used a fan. And she had a mouth with a mind of its own. 'How about an honest-to-goodness, no-holds-barred grovel?' he suggested.

'Will that do it?'

Well, she'd told him not to pretend . . . not that he needed the advice; the one thing she had learned about Nick Jefferson was that he said exactly what he thought. So it was stupid to be disappointed when he took her at her word.

He might be sitting beside her now, sharing a bottle of wine with her and quite prepared to advance the evening at whatever pace she dictated, but if he had conveniently forgotten the reason for his desperate telephone call she hadn't. And she wasn't about to let down her guard for something that meant nothing, no matter how unexpectedly her pulse might race at the thought. The fact that her pulse was racing was warning enough. Not all men were like Jonathan, but she knew better than to take the risk.

'Is impressing this woman so important to you?' she asked, reminding him of his purpose.

'I wouldn't be asking if it wasn't

important. So, do I grovel?'

'You could try,' Cassie quickly conceded, looking away. It would certainly be interesting to see how he went about it . . . she'd bet her last strand of saffron that he didn't have a lot of practice in grovelling. 'But you'll hate yourself afterwards for deceiving her.'

'Why don't you let me worry about that?'

He smiled so easily, Cassie thought. Well, she knew what that was worth. He wouldn't hate himself; he wouldn't give it a second thought. 'If this is so important to you, Nick, take the day off tomorrow, buy a cartload of chicken pieces and practise until you can cook the dish with your eyes closed. It isn't difficult, for heaven's sake. In fact it's about as easy as cooking gets.'

'Is that right?' He gave her the kind of look that suggested he thought she was spinning him a line. 'Well, I appreciate the advice, but I've got meetings all day tomorrow.'

'Cancel them.'

'Oh, sure,' he said, with deep irony. 'I'll send a memo, shall I? 'Hold the launch of the new golf range, folks, while I hone up my culinary skills.' That would go down a treat in the boardroom.'

'It would give them something interesting to talk about while they were waiting for you to turn up.'

'Yes,' he said, a touch dryly. 'I imagine it would.' He glanced down at her. 'Come on, Cassie, be a sport. Walk me through it.'

'Why?'

'You know why.'

Oh, yes, she knew why. What woman could resist a man who had gone to the trouble of cooking a special meal for her? It was so 'new man', so different. So appallingly cynical. 'No, I mean why are you putting yourself through this? No one, least of all some classy blonde, expects you to be able to cook.'

'It's complicated.'

'No, it isn't. It's very simple. The

truth of the matter, Nick, is that you're a grade A, free-range — '

'If I admit I'm a grade A . . . whatever,' he interrupted before she could read him his character, 'if I hold my hand up to being a prize idiot and confess that I've got myself into this mess for reasons that are not in the least bit noble . . . will that satisfy you?'

As grovelling went, it was a class act, she had to admit. But that was Nick Jefferson. A class act from start to finish. But an act, nevertheless. Which made it all the more urgent that she put a stop to the mad racketing in her circulatory system, the really crazy longing that Nick Jefferson would be prepared to go to so much trouble to . . . To what? To seduce *her*? Was that what she was wishing? Crazy was right.

'I'm sorry, Nick, I have a problem with this kind of thing. Something to do with being a clergyman's daughter, I expect. I'd really rather not get involved.' And she managed to ease herself away and put an inch between them. It wasn't enough. She could still feel the heat from his body, was still drowning in the scent of man-flesh with only the fresh, laundered smell of his T-shirt to distract her. And it wasn't. Distracting her. 'Would you move those peas for me?' she asked, quickly. So that he would have to move. 'They're defrosting all over Dem's favourite cushion.'

He didn't move, but continued to stare down at her with a slightly bemused expression. 'You're — '

'A prude? Oh, for goodness' sake, Nick, if you want to entice an attractive woman into your bed with the help of good food, a few glasses of wine and a romantic CD playing in the background, and if she's happy about it, I'm not about to throw a faint. I just don't want to be part of the orchestra.'

Jealous. That was what he'd been about to say. It had come to him in a blinding flash and he'd almost blurted it out. He must be losing his grip. Cassie would deny jealousy with her last breath. Who wouldn't? *Jealous*.

He smiled. 'I'm not asking you to play a violin, Cassie. Simply be there — '

'Be there! Skulking about in the kitchen while you romance some female out of her knickers — '

'Good grief, Cassie, what do you take me for?' As if he needed to ask — she'd made her opinion of him more than plain. 'On a first date?' And the last. He'd call it off now except that Veronica would look at him with that cool little smile and walk away the psychological winner.

She stared at him, through thick, dark lashes. 'This is really important to you?'

'I told you. Win or die in the attempt.'

'She must be very beautiful.'

Jealous. 'Veronica? Yes, she is. And very clever.' He saw her eyes spark. Gold glints in the butterscotch. And dark little patches of colour on her cheekbones. *Jealous as hell*. The knowledge gave him a warm feeling of satisfaction deep inside that he would take out and examine at his leisure later.

'She can't be that clever if she thinks you can cook.' *Veronica*. Even her name was long and glamorous, Cassie thought. 'So, why aren't you wooing this paragon with flowers and expensive restaurants instead of risking a fiasco?' she demanded.

His smile was the merest lifting of one corner of his mouth. Self-deprecating. A touch wry. 'Flowers and expensive restaurants are just so obvious. Don't you think?'

'Obvious. But rather nice. Occasionally,' she added, just in case he got the wrong idea. 'Or are you telling me that you think a walk along the beach in the rain is the height of romance?'

'Isn't it?' Nick, recognising a genuine fantasy when he heard it, filed that one away for future reference. After all, you never knew when a fantasy would come in handy. 'To be honest, Cassie, the choice of venue wasn't left to me. Veronica saw your cookery book on my desk and being a truthful man I had to admit that it was mine. And she invited herself to dinner.'

'You could have explained.'

'I could have. But it really was too good a chance to pass up. As I said, she's really very lovely. And until then she'd been playing hard to get.'

Cassie couldn't believe the man. He was just so ... so ... so ... *smug*. 'That's appalling, Nick — '

'I know. I struggled with my conscience ... ' the door-bell rang ' ... but not very hard. That'll be our supper.' He uncurled from the sofa and headed towards the stairs.

'Actually I don't think I'm that hungry any more.'

'Too late.'

'Oh, just go away, Nick, and take your Chinese takeaway with you,' she told him irritably.

'You don't mean that. Besides, I won't be able to eat it all.'

'Save what you can't eat for Veronica. She's going to need it,' Cassie declared. And when he laughed she leaned forward, picked up the pack of defrosting peas and flung it at him.

He fielded it without difficulty and placed it on the countertop. 'I'll pay you for your time,' he offered, quite deliberately turning the screw a little tighter. There was something about the way she sparked when she was angry that promised real fireworks if she ever lost control. And he loved fireworks.

'You couldn't afford me,' she declared. 'And even if you could I wouldn't take your money.'

'Who said anything about money? We'll talk terms over supper.' The doorbell sounded again, more impatiently this time. 'I'd better get that.'

'Get it and go,' Cassie shouted after him, but Nick was already thudding up the stairs to the front door and she wasn't under any illusion that he would do as she said.

She had his word that he never gave up until he got what he wanted. And he wanted her. Her help, she corrected herself. Her help. That was all.

7

Maybe that was the answer. If she ensured his seduction feast was a success then he would be too busy with Veronica to bother her again. And if he wasn't around she wouldn't have to keep battling with the disturbing feelings that he had brought bubbling to the surface. Feelings that she knew were much better kept, like secrets, safely buried where they could do no harm.

Very well. If that was what it took. But she wasn't going to let him think she was a pushover. It would take more than one little grovel and a pretty please to win her co-operation. After all, he had said he'd pay for her help and she had the feeling that she would be able to name her price. So what would it be? Not money. Money wouldn't hurt; he had too much of it. And she wanted him to hurt. But cosying up on the sofa wasn't doing anything for her thinking process.

Taking advantage of his absence, she swung herself round and lowered her undamaged foot to the floor. At least if she was sitting at the table she would have a chair all to herself, preferably with three feet of solid pine between them. Using the arm of the sofa, she hauled herself upright and very gingerly lowered her other toe to the floor. Her ankle complained. Loudly.

She really needed a stick, but since she didn't have one the furniture would have to do. She leaned across towards her desk, grasped the corner and took a small hop.

Pain scythed through her ankle as her body jarred against the floor, bringing an expletive surging to her lips. She bit them as the sweat beaded her forehead, refusing to utter a sound, no matter how much it hurt. But for a moment she didn't think she could make another move.

Yet the alternative was to have Nick find her swaying between the sofa and the desk. To have him help her back to the sofa. Mop her brow. Loosen her shirt, take her pulse again. The thought was so enticing, so real that she could almost feel those long fingers against her skin. *Too* enticing, *too* real. It was definitely time to move.

She swallowed hard. One hop to the edge of the countertop. One hop along it. Then the space across to the table — an empty space with nothing to cling onto. Concentrating on the goal of the chair, she took one little hop and, struggling for balance, she hung there with no support but her one good ankle.

Then she made the mistake of looking up.

*   *   *

Nick, having paid the delivery boy, was taking his time about returning to the kitchen, using the time to decide how he was going to persuade Cassie to help him. Because he hadn't been kidding when he'd said that winning was everything. He wasn't fooling himself either; to win he needed her help. In retrospect, however, he realised that it had been a mistake to offer to pay her.

It was fun to see her rise to his teasing, but he didn't want her mad, he wanted her co-operative. There must be something she wanted, something that he could do for her. She was going to need a driver if she was going to take her nephews away. And someone to erect the tent, organise the camp. He couldn't do it, of course. He was far too busy. But one of the young men who worked for him could be spared for a day. It would, after all, be an act of kindness . . . 'What on earth — ?'

Cassie, standing on one foot in the middle of the kitchen floor, was swaying dangerously. He dropped the carrier bag the delivery boy had given him and raced across the kitchen, catching her as she pitched forward into his arms.

She seemed incredibly small as he gathered her against him. Small and shapely, with a real old-fashioned waist that nipped in as if inviting an arm to slide about it. An invitation that he was happy to accept. She was the kind of woman built to sit on a man's lap and lie against his chest with her head tucked beneath his chin.

Maybe that was why he held onto her for longer than was strictly necessary to stop her from falling. Why he found himself scooping her up against his chest.

Why kissing her suddenly seemed like a thoroughly good idea.

'What the devil do you think you're doing?' Nick, trying to ignore a dozen signals flashing at him from every corner of his own body and quite a few of hers, heard himself growling at the woman.

Kissing Cassie might seem like a good idea and usually he wouldn't have thought twice about it. He hadn't thought twice about it in the bookshop.

After all, you only lived once and he hadn't had his face slapped . . . yet. But this time something stopped him. Some in-built sense of self-preservation warned him that Cassie didn't play those games. And he didn't play any other kind.

'Well?' he demanded, when she didn't answer him. 'Aren't you content with one twisted ankle? Are you going for the full set?'

'What's the matter, Nick?' Cassie responded, with equal vigour. 'Are you concerned that if I do any more damage I won't be fit to help you lay on the seduction feast?'

Anger would do as well as any other emotion to disguise the warm surge of desire that had swept over her as she had lain against Nick Jefferson's chest. The need simply to let go and have him hold her, kiss her, make love to her. Was she going out of her mind? Hadn't she learned her lesson? He might not be Jonathan's equal in the bastard stakes, but he would still use her and walk away and not look back.

It had been a long time since she had felt those kind of longings, yet the feelings had rushed back, clear and bright and urgent, as if it were the very first time. And how like her to choose the wrong man. Again.

Not that it mattered. She'd obviously misread the situation. No man who kissed girls as easily as Nick Jefferson would have missed out on that opportunity. Not with her positively panting to be kissed.

'Could you put me down, please, Nick? No, not on the sofa — ' But he wasn't listening. He crossed to the sofa and put her down on the soft cushions with a speed that suggested he couldn't wait to rid himself of an unwelcome burden. Dem, thoroughly fed up with being disturbed yet again, leapt to his paws, hackles raised, back arched, hissing furiously.

Nick looked down at him. Then he folded his long body until his face was level with that of the cat and Cassie drew in a sharp breath. 'What's bothering you, puss?' he demanded. For a moment Dem's golden eyes sparked venom but when Nick didn't back off the cat abruptly sat down and began to lick furiously at it's back.

Cassie let out the breath she had been holding. 'You've embarrassed him,' she said.

'I'm not surprised. He has appalling manners.'

'He's a male; what do you expect?'

For a moment Nick remained perfectly still, a tiny frown creasing the broad space between his brows. Then he stood up. 'Stay there, Cassie,' he said, his hand briefly touching her shoulder. 'I'll find some plates and be right back.'

Cassie considered telling him to forget it. Just to go away and leave her and Dem in peace. But since it would clearly be a total waste of breath she said, 'They're in the cupboard at the end . . . ' But he'd already found them. Cassie turned to Dem and let out a rather shaky breath, gently smoothing her hand over the cat's sleek coat. Dem gave her finger a quick sympathetic lick with his rough tongue and carried on washing. 'You'll find the forks . . . ' But he'd found them too and was busy opening the cartons of food.

'Shall I bring it all over or will you trust me to do this for you?' Nick asked, turning to her.

'What is it?'

'Duck. Do you want everything in your pancakes?'

'Why not?' She waited while he prepared a couple of pancakes and brought them over to her. 'I can't remember the last time I had a take-away,' she said.

He eased himself onto the sofa alongside her. 'I don't suppose it would do much for your reputation being seen dashing into fast-food joints. I don't suppose it's even close to your exalted standards . . . '

'On the contrary, it's delicious. Where did it come from?'

'The Lotus Flower.'

'The Lotus?' No wonder it tasted good. The Lotus Flower had more stars, medals, recommendations in good food guides than any other restaurant, Chinese or any other nationality, in the county. 'I didn't know they did take-away food.'

Nick shrugged. 'The owner owed me a favour. I found his daughter a tennis coach.' He caught her eye. 'She's eleven years old, Cassie, in case you were wondering ... and a first-rate tennis player.'

'It's none of my business how old she is.' Then she said, 'Maybe you should ask *him* to find you a cooking coach.'

'Why should I, when I've got you? More wine?' The phone began to ring. 'Shall I get that?' Before she could answer he had reached across and picked up the telephone. 'Melchester 690016.' He trotted out her number as casually as his own, Cassie fumed. 'Well, she's lying down right now; is it urgent?' Cassie practically threw herself

171

at him to get the phone, but he lifted it out of her reach and, not bothering to cover the receiver, said, 'It's someone called Matt. Do you want to speak to him? Or shall I ask him to call back in the morning?'

'Give me that telephone,' she whispered fiercely. He surrendered it with a grin, silently mouthing, 'Only joking,' as he did so. She glowered back. 'Matt? What can I do for you?'

Her brother-in-law chuckled. 'Tell me if I'm disturbing something here, Cassie, and I'll call back when you aren't so, er, busy.'

'I'm not in the least bit busy,' she declared, glaring at Nick. 'What's up?'

'Nothing new. I just wanted to warn you that Lauren is still trying to wriggle out of this trip to Portugal.' His voice lost all trace of laughter. 'I think she'd use any excuse — '

'Then don't give her one.'

'No, you don't understand. She's using you. She keeps saying that you won't be able to cope with the boys

172

. . . that I shouldn't have insisted on you going to Morgan's Landing . . . you know, the same old stuff . . . '

'You've had another row?'

'You could say that. Anyone would think I enjoy working fourteen hours a day.'

'Maybe it's easier than coming home these days?'

'I have to earn a living.'

'You do a lot more than that. But when you've made your first million and you're living in luxury will it be worth a broken marriage and seeing the boys once a week?' There was silence from the other end of the phone. 'You're going to have to sort out your priorities, you know. You can't go on like this. Lauren won't put up with it.'

'She was the one who wanted the big new house, a car of her own, private schools for the kids . . . '

'Not at the expense of your marriage. Talk to her, Matt. Tell her how you feel.' He was silent. 'Try and remember what it was like before you started giving

Lauren *things* instead of yourself,' she urged. 'I scarcely qualify as an agony aunt and my own marriage was too short to provide much of an example — ' not one that anyone would want to emulate, anyway ' — but I do know that it has to be worked at.'

'Have you told *her* that?'

'It doesn't matter who makes the first move. Just so long as someone does.'

'You should have got married again, Cass; you know all the answers.' *Oh, sure.* 'What about the guy who answered the phone? Any chance?'

'None whatever. I'll expect the boys first thing on Friday morning,' she continued, briskly changing the subject. 'Actually, you'd better make some excuse to bring them yourself.'

'Why?'

'I had a bit of an accident. Nothing much. But if Lauren sees me hobbling . . . '

'Hobbling? Oh, God, this is going to be a disaster, I know it.'

'It's just a twisted ankle,' she

declared. 'Nothing to worry about. But well . . . you said it. Best not to give Lauren any excuse.'

'You're sure?'

'Try and stop me.'

'Thanks, Cass. You're a brick.'

'You're the builder, so I guess you should know.'

'Your brother?' Nick enquired as he took the receiver from Cassie and replaced it on the hook. He was looking at her curiously and she knew he'd picked up on the fact that she had been married, noted that she wasn't wearing a ring. She'd seen that speculative look before, on the face of men who were trying to decide whether she was a merry widow or a gay divorcée — and trying to work out how long it would take to get her into bed.

'Brother-in-law,' she said quickly before he could ask.

'And father of the three young hunks you're taking camping?' Nick saw a look of something like panic cross her face. She expected him to ask about her husband and she didn't want to talk about it. He wondered why. 'I got the drift of why you volunteered, but just how do you think you're going to manage?'

'I'll manage,' she assured him.

'How?' he persisted.

'I'll think of something.'

'There's no need to strain your brain, Cassie, I've already come up with a solution.'

'Have you? Why should you worry about my problems?' He shrugged. 'Well?' Nick took his time about finishing his pancake. Then he licked his fingers, took a sip of wine. 'Nick!'

'Someone has to. Here's the deal. I'll provide you with a driver and someone to set up camp for you, make sure you've got everything you need. And he'll come and bring you home whenever you want.'

'And why will you do that?'

'Guilty conscience, perhaps?' he suggested, nodding towards her ankle. 'There are several junior execs at

Jefferson Sports just dying to prove their initiative. They'll just jump at the chance to help you out.'

'Really? Jump, you say?' Her brows contracted in an ironic little frown. 'Are you certain of that? It sounds as if they'll be pushed to me, which begs the question, what will you get out of this, Nick?' As if she didn't know. 'I just don't buy the guilty conscience bit.'

'No?' He grinned, not the least bit ashamed. 'Then what about your help with a little cooking?'

He looked far too pleased with himself for Cassie's liking. He thought she was going to fall over herself to accept his offer, but she'd done all the falling she was going to do for one night.

'Let's get this straight, Nick. You want me to cook a seduction feast for you and in return you'll provide me with someone to take me to Wales and set up camp?'

'It seems a fair exchange to me.'

'But you have a vested interest.

177

Frankly, I think I'd rather pay someone to do it.'

'Some stranger? Out in the wilds? With you hobbling about on a stick and three small boys to take care of?'

Put like that it did sound less than ideal, but she wasn't to be bought quite that easily. 'Your man would be a stranger, too,' she pointed out.

'A vouched-for, vetted and terribly keen stranger. And absolutely guaranteed to know one end of a tent from the other.'

Cassie found herself wavering. She hated conspiring with the wretched man in such blatant deceit, but she wasn't kidding herself about the fact that she did need help. And if, by cooking dinner for Veronica, she could prove to herself and Nick Jefferson that she didn't care one jot for the way he behaved, well, that had to be a good thing, didn't it?

And presumably Veronica, once seduced, would keep him fully occupied. It never occurred to her that he might fail.

Nick smiled as he saw her determination begin to crumble. 'Well, do we have a deal?' He offered up his wine glass.

She touched it with her own. 'It's a deal,' she agreed.

'Good. Now tell me about this husband of yours. Did he jump or was he pushed?'

Cassie gasped. Was that his technique? Lull a girl into a false sense of security and then — *wham*. He was waiting for an answer. Well, he could have one. She gave him a shove that took him by surprise and sent him flying off the sofa so that the wine shot over his face and ran down his neck.

'Does that answer your question?' she demanded.

'I guess so,' he said, exposing a washboard-flat stomach as he tugged out the tail of his T-shirt to dry his face.

'Good. Now go home, Nick,' Cassie said irritably. 'You've worn out your welcome.'

* * *

Nick picked her up at six the following evening and drove her to a small village just outside the city. Cassie was determined to be utterly professional about this evening, but she couldn't help but be impressed by his home. Beth had said it was lovely and she hadn't exaggerated.

It was a low, ground-hugging, thatched cottage, genuinely oak-beamed and white-washed, which had started out as a row of smaller cottages but had, at some time, been converted into one big house that meandered unevenly alongside a quiet country lane. But if the outside was all olde-worlde charm, the inside was not.

'Goodness,' Cassie said as she stood in the kitchen doorway. 'This is . . . un-expected.'

'I know. It doesn't quite go with the house does it?'

'You said it. Who perpetrated this crime?' she said, remembering too late the glamorous decorator.

'An interior designer I knew.'

Cassie gave him an old-fashioned look. 'A tall, blonde designer?' she enquired.

Nick shrugged. 'She needed somewhere to try out a few ideas. This place was a bit of a mess when I bought it and since I didn't have any time for decorating I left her to get on with it.'

'I hope she was suitably grateful.'

'Let's just say it was a mutually rewarding relationship that ran its natural course.'

Cassie limped into the dining room. Grey, black and chrome. 'She wasn't out of the frills and flowers school of interior design, was she?' He shrugged. 'Beth thought you might have bought this place with something more permanent in mind,' she said, looking around.

'Did she?' They'd talked about him, then? 'No. The lease was about to expire on my flat and it was a good time to buy. I liked this place on sight.' He followed her disparaging glance. 'Do you want to see the rest of it?'

She tried to imagine his bedroom.

Concealed lighting, a black carpet and a wolfskin bedcover? 'No, thanks.'

He grinned. 'You're right. I'll have to get someone who knows what she's doing to sort it out.' He put his hand beneath her elbow. 'Come on. Better get the weight off that foot. Then you can show me what to do.'

'*You?*' she said, disparagingly enough to distract herself from thinking about his arm on her elbow. 'I thought *I* was here to do the cooking.'

'You're just here to make sure I don't make any mistakes. I want to be able to look Veronica in the eye and say I cooked this.'

'Right.' That sounded more like a challenge accepted and answered than a prelude to seduction. But whatever turned you on.

It was comfortable working in the kitchen with Cassie for company, Nick thought, despite the chill efficiency of the decor. She carried her own warmth about with her and, propped on a stool at the central island, she told him about working in television, the disasters as well as the triumphs, sparing herself not at all as he grated and chopped to her instructions. He noticed she steered well clear of her personal life.

'Don't get any of the white pith in with the lemon rind,' she warned as he attacked it with the rough side of the grater. 'It'll make the dish taste bitter.'

'But nothing happens if I use the fine cutter,' he protested.

'All you need is the zest, the oil from the skin and the magic happens. Now squeeze the juice and everything is ready.'

'What about the stock?'

'I brought a pint of my own.'

'Did you? But isn't that — ?'

'Yes?'

'Cheating?'

'Probably, but I won't tell if you don't.'

He shrugged. 'Well, I hope it's a good one.'

She glared at him. 'It's in my basket. Pass it to me, will you?' He lifted the small round old-fashioned basket she had brought with her onto the counter-top and she took out a screw-topped jar and poured the liquid into a measuring jug. 'Now hadn't you better go and lay the table?'

'Yes, ma'am.'

'And don't forget flowers for the table,' she called after him.

He did a double take. 'Flowers?'

'You forgot.' She shook her head. 'Pick a few from the garden. You've got a red rose climbing through that old apple tree out the back; that'll do.'

'Red roses are a bit — ' He stopped, made a helpless little gesture that was unusually awkward for him. Embarrassed even.

'Obvious?' she offered.

'A bit too much of a statement.'

'And you wouldn't want to give the poor woman the impression that you really cared? You're right, yellow would look better with all that grey.' And in the language of flowers implied insincerity, but she didn't tell him that.

'Shall I assemble your starter while you're doing that?'

He glanced at his watch. 'Would you mind? I'm running out of time and I need to take a shower — ' He broke off. 'Will you stop looking at me like that?'

'Like what?'

'As if you want to laugh, but you're being too damned polite.'

'Oh. Sorry. I'll try and take this seriously. Give me a hand down, will you?'

He crossed the kitchen and, ignoring her extended hand, he put his hands about her waist and lifted her off the stool, placing her very gently on the floor.

'Thank you,' she said, with just a hint of a catch in her throat.

'You're welcome.' Damn, damn, damn. Why on earth had he got himself into this mess? He didn't want Veronica Grant at his table, he wanted Cassie. He wanted her so badly that if he didn't let her go right now, walk away and take a cold shower, he would do something really stupid. Like telling her that he loved her. Which was ridiculous. He didn't go in for such rubbish. Good grief, he scarcely knew anything about her. Except that once she was married and now she was not. And she didn't like to talk about it.

'Go on,' she said, giving him a little push. 'Your blonde telegraph pole will be here soon. No, wait. You'd better show me where I'm going to hide if she comes snooping in the kitchen to check up on you.'

He looked genuinely startled. 'She won't, will she?'

'She might,' Cassie warned. Nick dragged his fingers through his hair and she was glad he was finding this deception more difficult than he'd expected. It made him seem just a little nicer. Which on top of the charm and the smile was really more than she could deal with. 'I would,' she added.

'Well, there's a pantry. Through there,' he said, opening a door to expose an old-fashioned pantry lined with unused shelves that made her practically drool with longing to fill it with preserves and jams.

'And where does that door lead to?' she asked, indicating another door alongside it.

'The mud room, then the garden,' he said, showing her. The manic decorator hadn't got this far. The worn quarry tiles were old and the walls had been painted cream a long time ago. A lonely and very shabby waxed jacket hung from a row of hooks, and on the floor beneath it was a pair of wellington boots that looked as if they had never encountered a puddle in their life, let alone mud. 'I thought I might try my hand at gardening, but I don't seem to have much time,' Nick said, reading her expression with alarming accuracy.

'Well, at least I'll be able to get out without your guest seeing me,' Cassie said, opening a door to disclose a loo and washbasin. A second door opened on a narrow flight of stairs. 'I'd better be out of here before the real reason for this evening gets under way,' she said.

'Cassie!'

'What?' Butter wouldn't have melted in her mouth.

'Those are the back stairs. The main staircase is — ' He realised she had been teasing him and stopped.

'Regular servants' quarters,' she said. 'How appropriate.' Something very like a blush darkened his cheekbones, probably for the first time since he had outgrown puberty. 'Don't worry, Nick, the minute dinner is served I intend to get out of here.' She might have been kidding him but she had a pretty good idea what would happen once the after-dinner mints had been consumed and she didn't plan to stick around and have her suspicions confirmed. 'Did you arrange a taxi for me?'

'Yes, but I wasn't sure what time it would be needed . . . you just have to call the number by the phone when you're ready. It's all paid for.' He hesitated. 'I haven't thanked you properly for saving my skin, Cassie.'

'Don't worry, I'm sure your young man has been instructed to do that most efficiently on your behalf.' Her mouth-only smile indicated that she considered this cheap of him, but since she really wasn't in a position to turn his offer down she didn't push it. 'Now, don't you think you'd better go and make yourself beautiful before your date arrives?' she said, her sweetness so false that it was positively saccharine. 'It's always difficult to look your best when you've been slaving over a hot stove, but you wouldn't want Veronica to think you hadn't made an effort, would you?'

Veronica Grant was not a date, she was a challenge. But Nick knew that saying so would do nothing to improve Cassie's opinion of him. The truth was that his own opinion of himself wasn't all that high right now. Veronica was a brilliant marketing professional and if he messed up their working relationship because of some stupid bet on the men's-room wall . . . Beth was right; it was definitely time he grew up. And now would be a good time to start.

Veronica had invited herself to dinner and dinner was all she was going to get. As for Cassie, well, he needed to take a little time to think about why her opinion mattered so much. It was too important to get it wrong.

'Can I get you a drink before I go?' he offered.

'Only male television cooks can get away with drinking on the job, Nick,' she replied. Which was rather a pity. She had the feeling that a drink or two would have gone a long way to helping her through the next hour or so.

8

She couldn't wait for Nick to go, to have the kitchen to herself, yet the minute he had gone Cassie missed him. Which was idiotic. He didn't care two hoots about her, or about anyone but himself. He wasn't even putting himself out to thank her for helping him. He was getting someone else to do his dirty work, something he was very good at, she decided as she arranged curls of smoked salmon and unshelled prawns on two plates with elaborate care. Added a twist of lemon peel and cucumber.

It wasn't as if he was making any pretence about it. He was having this meal with another woman, after all. One of those leggy blondes he found so appealing.

'Everything under control?' She was mixing the flavourings with the mayonnaise when Nick put one hand on her shoulder and leaned over to hook a finger through the mixture and taste it. She slapped irritably at the back of his hand with a spoon. 'More mustard,' he said.

'Who's making this mayonnaise?' she demanded.

'Me,' Nick reminded her. 'At least in theory. And I'd definitely use more mustard.' He offered her his finger to lick. He had long fingers. Strong, straight with smooth, sensitive tips. She swallowed and dolloped in another spoonful of mustard.

'I'll take your word for it,' she said, whisking the mayonnaise with consider-ably more force than was necessary. His other hand was still on her shoulder and she turned to glance at his watch. His wrist was thick and sinewy with a generous sprinkling of sun-lightened hair, the wrist of a man who played tennis or golf. Very well. The kind of wrist a woman would enjoy rubbing her cheek against. When she wasn't licking his fingers.

She closed her eyes. What on earth

was happening to her? Five years without so much as a flicker of temptation to divert her. Now one kiss from Nick Jefferson had woken up all those little slumbering memories of how it was to be touched, stroked, kissed, loved . . . 'What time is Veronica due?' she asked, in an endeavour to keep her mind on food.

'Any minute.'

'Let's get started, then. You want her to smell something cooking when she arrives or she'll think you've just heated it up in the microwave. Put on the oven.' She slid off the stool, wincing slightly as her foot touched the ground, and then produced a pack of cook-at-home rolls from her basket and handed them to him. 'I'd normally make my own bread, but frankly I think you'd be pushing credibility a touch too far if you tried to get away with that one. But if you put these in the oven it will give the place a homey smell.'

'Like people do when they're selling a house?' He didn't move. 'No one falls for that one, surely?'

'Just put them on a tray, Nick. In the oven. It'll tell you on the packet what temperature.' He still didn't move. 'What is it?' she asked.

'I'm not sure I can do this.' He took in the kitchen with a broad gesture. 'I'll have to tell her.'

After all the trouble she'd gone to? 'Oh, come on, Nick. Pretending that you've suddenly developed a conscience isn't going to impress me one bit.' The doorbell rang. 'Hadn't you better answer that? You can worry about your conscience — and the risk of blackmail — in the morning. I'm sure it will be worth it.'

'Blackmail?' He still hadn't moved.

'Go,' she said, waving him away. 'I was just kidding. I won't tell a soul about this; I've got my own reputation to think about, you know. The tabloids would have a field day if they ever found out about this. And since I don't for one minute believe that you have a conscience — '

'Kidding again?' he cut in, his mouth tight, his eyes quite suddenly about as warm as agate.

She glanced up at him, surprised that he had taken offence. 'I guess I just can't help myself.' But she wasn't about to apologise. 'Now, if you'll just try and keep her out of the kitchen . . . ' He was still staring at her. He was that angry? 'I'm sure you can think of some way of distracting her,' Cassie added, a touch recklessly, anything to get him to move.

'I'm sure I can,' Nick replied, a dangerous edge to his voice. And as the bell pealed again he spun round and walked out of the kitchen. Well, that was what she had wanted, wasn't it?

Cassie shut her ears to the sounds coming from the front hall and put the heat under the frying-pan. Half an hour and she would be out of here, she promised herself. And she promised whichever saint was responsible for the welfare of cooks that she would never, ever, do anything like this again. Honest.

* * *

'Veronica, how lovely to see you.' Nick invested his voice with special warmth, just in case Cassie happened to be listening. Although why she would be he couldn't imagine. She'd made it quite clear that he was one step up from a louse. Or maybe she didn't consider that he was that high on the evolutionary scale.

'Oh, I wouldn't have missed this for the world, Nick.' Veronica stepped into the hall, looking about her. He took her wrap and led her into the living room which suddenly seemed to have too much new black leather and not enough genuine comfort. 'Nice house,' she said politely.

'It needs some work,' he said, not bothering to explain that none of this was his choice. He didn't actually care very much what Veronica thought of his home. In fact he couldn't wait to get her out of it. 'Can I get you a drink?'

'A glass of wine, please. White.

Something dry?'

'No problem. Make yourself at home.'

She remained on her feet. 'Can I look around?'

He remembered Cassie's warning that Veronica would be on the prowl. 'Help yourself,' he said, after the briefest pause. 'I'll get you a drink and check on things in the kitchen.'

He pushed the door open, but the kitchen was empty, with only the gentle sizzle of meat in the pan to reassure him that Cassie was about somewhere. He took a bottle of Chardonnay from the fridge and peeled away the foil from the cork. Then he glanced anxiously at the pan, remembering how quickly everything had gone ballistic when he'd tried cooking the dish himself. She might think him a louse but she wouldn't have walked out and left him, would she?

'Cassie?' The pantry door opened a fraction and she peered round it, her face slightly flushed, her hair already slipping from its pins. Unlike Veronica, who never had a hair out of place, Cassie couldn't seem to control the sleek heavy mass of her hair. He wanted to reach out and tuck it back in place; his fingers curled with the sheer effort of not doing it. 'What on earth are you doing in there?'

'What do you think I'm doing?' she demanded in a fierce whisper. 'Hiding from your seducee.'

'My what?'

Not entirely confident that there was such a word, Cassie couldn't bring herself to repeat it. 'I nearly broke my neck getting in here. Couldn't you have whistled or something to warn me that you were coming?'

'I think Veronica might just be a little suspicious if I did that, don't you?' He had the feeling she was suspicious anyway. 'Besides, I was on my own.'

'I didn't know that — '

'You can see through the ventilation holes — ' he glanced at the door with its three-inch-wide holes drilled three-quarters of the way up the door ' — if you stand on tiptoe — '

'Nick?' Veronica's voice wafted down the corridor.

'I'm in the kitchen.' Reassured that she was still on his side, no matter how reluctantly, Nick grinned at Cassie. 'If you don't want to get caught, you'd better do your disappearing act again,' he advised.

Cassie glared at him. 'Put the lemon in,' she whispered urgently. 'Now.' And dived back into the pantry as Veronica appeared in the doorway.

'My goodness. What a hive of domesticity.' Nick was saved from answering by the hiss and sizzle of the lemon juice hitting the pan. 'Can I do anything?'

'If you like. You'll find a couple of plates of smoked salmon in the fridge. You could take them into the dining room for me while I open this wine.'

'Smoked salmon?' She opened the fridge. 'And strawberries, too. How lovely.'

'And how easy?'

'I wouldn't dream of saying that.'

'No, but you were thinking it,' he said, as she passed him with the salmon. He finished opening the wine and poured it into two glasses.

Cassie put her head round the door. 'Has she gone?'

'Only for a minute.'

'Quick, put in the rosemary and give it a stir.'

He crossed to the hob and did as she said. 'Then what?'

'Then what, what?' Veronica asked. He spun round to find her leaning against the island, sipping at her wine. He had to make a real effort not to look back towards the pantry.

'Uh . . . I was just talking to myself. I've put in the rosemary, but I can't remember which comes next, the stock or the soured cream . . . ' He smiled as if the answer had suddenly come to him. 'The stock.' The jug with the measured amount was standing beside the hob. He poured it in and, improvising, gave it a stir.

'What is it?' she asked, leaning over the hob. 'Oh, chicken. Well, it smells delicious.'

'Let's hope it tastes as good,' he said, reaching for his glass.

'Don't you know?' Veronica was regarding him rather as a cat might have watched a bird he was planning to have for his supper, weighing the exact moment to strike. And he remembered feeling exactly the same way in the boardroom a few days earlier. What was she up to?

'Actually I don't. It's the first time I've . . . er . . . tried this particular dish.'

'And home-made bread, too,' she said.

'Bread?' Nick suddenly remembered the rolls. 'Oh, yes. But not home-made; I haven't got to that stage yet.' He put down his glass and retrieved the rolls from the oven, popping them quickly into a basket that had magically appeared. 'This is just good old 'take-and-bake',' he continued, marvelling at the way Cassie seemed to think of everything, have it to hand just at the moment it was needed. But then she was a professional. 'But give me time.' Behind Veronica's back, Nick could see Cassie's hand frantically waving around the pantry door, urging him from the kitchen.

'I'll just turn this down a little and we can go and start eating. If you're hungry?'

'Well, I did consider stopping off for a hamburger on the way. Just in case,' Veronica admitted. 'I didn't really think you could do this.' She looked around, still not totally convinced.

'No?' He encouraged her towards the dining room. 'Just wait. You ain't seen nothing yet.' And with that he glanced back at the pantry door and winked.

★ ★ ★

Cassie, her heart beating like an electric food mixer in overdrive — probably something to do with having to grit her teeth to repress a desperate urge to

202

scream — returned to the kitchen.

She placed the washed rice in a bowl ready for the microwave and firmly resisted the temptation to clear away and wash up while she waited for the kettle to boil. She was the cook, not the bottle-washer. Besides, Nick would have a job explaining a magical clear-up job to Veronica.

From her vantage point behind the pantry door she had had a good look at Nick's beautiful blonde and she didn't look like the kind of woman who believed in fairies.

Cassie checked the chicken for tenderness. It was just about done. She should have reminded Nick to pop back into the kitchen while his guest was busy with her smoked salmon before she moved on to the next stage of cooking. If Veronica was the kind of guest who liked to 'help', or if she had any lingering suspicions about Nick's probity, she would certainly follow him out into the kitchen and she would notice if the chicken had disappeared from the pan while they ate their salmon.

Like a gift from heaven, the kettle began to whistle. Loudly.

'No, you can't do a thing, Veronica. Just take your time. I won't be a minute.' Nick's voice carried to the kitchen. He followed it. 'What the hell was that?' he whispered furiously.

'The kettle. You put it on last time you were in here, don't you remember?' He gave her an old-fashioned look. 'Time to put on the rice,' she murmured as she poured on the boiling water and set the microwave. 'Make yourself useful if you're stopping, Nick. Take the chicken out of the pan and put it on that dish.'

He stuck a fork into the meat and lifted it onto the plate. 'Damn!' he said as he splashed the juice on his shirt. Cassie silently handed him a cloth.

'Don't worry, it'll lend you credibility,' she said, with the sweetest smile.

'Are you sure there's nothing I can do, Nick?' Veronica called.

'No. Just relax; I'll be right there,' he called, avoiding Cassie's eye. 'Oh, God, this is a nightmare. I'm beginning to sound just like my mother at Christmas.'

'Just as long as you don't start singing carols,' Cassie said, turning the heat up under the pan juices. 'Off you go. You've been in here quite long enough. You don't want her to come looking for you.' Or maybe he did. Maybe he really was suffering from a guilty conscience. 'I don't want her to find me, Nick.'

He grabbed the wine bottle from the island. Then, while she was too busy to realise what he was about, he bent and planted a kiss on Cassie's flushed cheek. 'Thank you, Cassie.'

Startled, she turned to him. Nose to nose, mouth to mouth they stared at one another. Then he kissed her again, hard and full on her mouth.

She was still standing, too shocked for words, as he disappeared through the kitchen door.

How dared he? How dared he kiss her, when he was going to such pains to romance another woman, a woman he clearly intended to give the grand tour of his pretty-on-the-outside, horrible-on-the-inside house, a tour that would undoubtedly end in his undoubtedly tasteless bedroom?

She lifted her hand to her mouth and wiped the back of it over her lips. Then she had to clench it to stop it from shaking.

Damn the man. And damn his arrogance. It would serve him right if she walked out right now and left him to finish cooking his own dinner. Instead she vented her spleen on a dozen white grapes, slicing angrily through them and gouging out the seeds while she waited for the juices to reduce in the pan. Cassie was still staring at the sauce when Nick walked in with the used plates. She said something very rude and dashed towards the pantry, ignoring the sharp jab of pain warning her that her ankle was not to be treated in such a cavalier fashion.

'Don't worry,' he said, catching her arm as she stumbled. 'Veronica's looking for a CD to put on. We've got a minute.'

She glared at him, jerked her arm away and pushed back a wayward strand of hair. 'In that case you'd better check the rice to see if it's done while I finish the chicken.' She swung away from him and concentrated very hard on warming through the chicken breasts and grapes in the sauce.

'This rice is done,' he said, making her jump. 'I'll put it in the serving dish, shall I?'

She turned to him. 'Nick — '

He glanced up. 'Yes?'

'Nothing.' Asking a man why he'd kissed you was not likely to produce a sensible answer. And it would suggest it mattered. Which it didn't. Mustn't. Couldn't. Instead she placed the chicken breasts on two plates and spooned the sauce over them. She added a tiny garnish of grapes and lemon peel.

'Cassie, this isn't . . . that is, I'm not — '

'Aren't you?' She squared up to him, hands on her hips. 'What's the matter with you, Nick? Isn't one woman enough for you?'

'Nick . . . ' Veronica's voice had the lilting, teasing note of a girl who just couldn't wait.

'Better not keep the lady waiting,' she said, turning away from him. 'It sounds to me as if you've hit pay dirt.'

'Damn it, Cassie — '

'Careful. She'll hear you.' She picked up the plates and pushed them into his hands. They were hot; she was used to that, he was not and she saw him wince. 'Go and eat your chicken before it gets cold,' she told him.

'Fat chance,' he muttered. 'What about the rice?'

'You'll have to come back for it. Unless you've got three hands?'

'With two women to keep happy I'll

need them, won't I?'

He hadn't got two women, Cassie thought furiously, but he didn't hang around long enough for her to say so, which was perhaps just as well. And she kept her head down when he returned for the rice, busily laying out the strawberries, chantilly cream and the special meringues she had made that morning on a tray.

What was it about the man that was so unsettling her? She had a busy life. A fulfilling career. Pretty much everything she could want. She'd done the love thing and, discovering that it wasn't all it was cracked up to be, she'd vowed never to be taken in by a man ever again. Particularly a man like Nick Jefferson. A cuckoo.

Cassie tried hard to ignore the soft murmur of voices seeping into the kitchen from the dining room over the elegant strains of Mozart's clarinet concerto. She tried hard not to think about what Nick was saying, what he might be doing.

She'd had her chance. Lunch at a restaurant of her choosing instead of slaving over a hot stove for some other woman. And she'd made the right choice. She didn't need a man to make her complete. Certainly not a man like Nick Jefferson. Been there, done that. Had the broken heart to prove it. Damn!

She dashed away a tear and added coffee cups to the tray, along with the cream and sugar. Nick had bought a box of expensive chocolate mints. She opened it and, feeling unbelievably miserable, she ate two. They didn't help and the gaps she had left in the box glared accusingly up at her. She tipped the rest of the mints out into a small glass dish she found in a cupboard. And, since Veronica clearly had never eaten chocolate in her life and wouldn't miss it, she ate another one. It just made her feel worse.

Then she heard movement in the dining room. Sick of hiding in the pantry, she fled to the loo. At least in there she could sit down and have a good cry if she wanted to. Not that she did, she told herself firmly, sniffing as quietly as she could.

'Idiot,' she muttered, confronting her reflection in the mirror and a pair of over-bright eyes. She sniffed again. Tore off half a yard of loo roll and blew her nose as quietly as she knew how. Then she splashed her face with cold water and reminded herself very firmly that two kisses meant nothing to a man like Nick Jefferson. It was just a hobby with him. Some men played cricket, or fished. He kissed women. Rumour had it that he preferred tall, blonde women, but it seemed that anything would do at a pinch.

When she finally emerged from the mud room, the tray with the strawberries and the coffee had gone and it was time for her to be gone too. Her ankle, which firm strapping and pain-killers had kept down to a bearable ache for most of the day, was beginning to throb and she limped across to the phone and dialled the number on a little yellow note stuck to the wall. It seemed to ring for ever.

'Come on,' she urged the inanimate receiver, desperate to get away. If she wasn't here she wouldn't have to think about Nick and Veronica lingering over coffee and brandy. She could pretend that Veronica had called for a taxi and gone home at a respectable hour. Fat chance.

'Melchester Taxis,' a voice finally informed her. She asked for a taxi and was told that they were busy, that it would take about twenty minutes to get to her. She was furious with herself for not anticipating how long it might take. But there was nothing she could do except wait.

The clock on the wall seemed to stand still. Only the occasional burst of laughter from the dining room punctuated seconds that moved like minutes, minutes that moved like hours.

Five minutes. Then ten. Eleven. Twelve. Cassie slid off the stool and decided that she would rather wait outside than endure another second in Nick's kitchen, listening to the murmur of voices while Nick wooed the fair Veronica.

The back door was bolted and the bolt was old and stiff. She bent down to work at it, fiddling it up and down. She was still trying to slide it back when she heard Veronica's high heels tapping across the ceramic tiles of the kitchen floor. 'Of course I must help you to wash up,' she declared, in clear, bright tones that seemed so close she might almost have been in the mud room with Cassie. 'It's the least I can do after such a wonderful meal.'

'There's no need, really,' Nick protested. 'I have someone who comes in to clean. She'll do it in the morning.'

'That's disgusting. Only a man would leave washing-up overnight for someone else. It won't take a moment.' There was the sound of running water. 'You make a start, Nick. I'll just use your loo and then I'll dry up.' Oh, neat.

That way she won't be the one with dish-pan hands. Cassie, infinitely cheered by the thought of Nick up to his elbows in dish water, straightened from her efforts with the bolt. And with Veronica upstairs she could slip out. 'Just point me in the right direction.'

'There's one through there.'

Through there? Through where? In answer to her silent question the mud-room door began to open.

Oh, good grief, he thought she'd already gone. Cassie gave the bolt one last desperate tug. It gave a loud squeal as she lifted the slider, but still refused to budge.

Had Veronica heard? Apparently not. But Nick must have, because she heard him move quickly across the kitchen. 'Actually, that one is a bit basic,' he said. 'Maybe you'd be more comfortable upstairs, Veronica.'

Veronica had a silvery laugh. 'For goodness' sake, Nick, don't make such a fuss. Basic is fine.'

'There might not be a towel,' he

improvised. 'Or soap. I'd better check.'

'Heavens, Nick, anyone would think you'd got something to hide. Skeletons in the ... um ... closet.' Nick obligingly laughed at her little joke. 'You haven't got a cordon bleu chef tucked away in there by any chance, have you?'

'A chef?' Nick managed to laugh at that, too. But to Cassie's ears not quite so convincingly. 'How suspicious you are, Veronica. If that's what you think, you'd better go ahead and look for yourself.'

At that point Cassie stopped eaves-dropping and took the only way out that was left to her. She slipped off her shoes, opened the door to the stairs and, ignoring her protesting ankle, fled up them.

9

Standing in the kitchen, contemplating a sink full of dirty dishes and wondering just how quickly he could persuade his unwanted guest to leave, Nick Jefferson had an idea.

He had just finished his call when he heard something unexpected and as he hung up he lifted his head and stared at the ceiling. There was someone upstairs, walking across the creaking old floorboards.

Cassie?

He had assumed she was long gone. She'd made her feelings plain enough so it seemed obvious that she would beat a retreat the minute she was free. So why was she still here?

He opened the mud-room door, planning a quick dash upstairs to find out what was happening, but Veronica was ahead of him, peering up the stairway. Had she heard Cassie, too?

'Two sets of stairs, Nick?' she enquired, turning to him, her face giving nothing away. But then it never did. Unlike Cassie, whose eyes betrayed everything she was thinking. Or almost everything. Questions about her husband just provoked a blankness. The hurt, whatever it was, was buried too deep to be teased out of her.

He smiled briefly. 'Of course, Veronica. One for going up and one for coming down.' She gave him an old-fashioned look and he shrugged. 'There were a lot more originally. One for each of the cottages. This one was left when the place was converted a few years ago by someone with a couple of children. So that they wouldn't traipse mud through the house.'

'Good thinking. Can I go up?' His brain seemed to be on some kind of a 'go slow', refusing to come up with some reasonable excuse to stop her. 'You did say I could look around.'

He shrugged. 'Sure. I'll show you

around when we've done the washing-up.'

'That'll keep.' She extended her hand. 'Come on.'

He looked at the hand, the slightly teasing smile that lifted the corners of her mouth, her eyes. A week ago he'd have accepted such an invitation without a second thought. Too late he discovered that he preferred Veronica cool and distant. 'You'd be safer going up the main staircase in those heels,' he said. 'This one's a bit . . . worn.'

'No problem.' She kicked off her shoes and since he hadn't taken her hand she grasped his and set off up the stairs. He had no choice but to follow her and hope the creaking would warn Cassie that they were on their way.

*   *   *

Cassie had been standing at the top of the stairs surveying the confusing layout of narrow corridors, the seemingly endless numbers of doors and wishing she'd taken the guided tour Nick had offered so that she could find her way to the main staircase and escape. All she could do was wait for Veronica to leave the mud room. Except she didn't.

She listened with growing concern to the other woman. Nick's voice was muffled, but it didn't take much imagination to know what his answer would be as Veronica invited herself upstairs. As they began to mount the stairs, she fled down the nearest corridor, desperately looking for the main staircase.

'This place is so quaint, Nick. What's that old rhyme? 'There was a crooked man and he built a crooked house . . . ''

'I don't think it goes quite like that.'

'No? Oh, well . . . ' She apparently stopped to look out of the small round window at the top of the stairs. 'And what a lovely garden. Is that another of your unexpected hobbies?'

'Veronica — '

'Is that a Bourbon rose? That pink one?'

'I don't know. I don't have time for gardening. Someone comes in once a week to keep it tidy.'

Their voices were terribly close and Cassie abandoned her search for the stairs and opened the first door she came to, desperately hoping it wasn't a cupboard. It wasn't. She stepped inside, pressing her back to the door while she gathered her breath. Then she looked around and barely choked back a groan.

It was Nick's bedroom. It had to be. The bed was huge and low, the sheets were black, the carpet pale grey. The monochrome designer had struck again. But at least her worst nightmare wasn't realised. The bed was not covered with some exotic animal skin but with a perfectly ordinary duvet, covered by a perfectly ordinary black duvet cover. If black bedlinen could ever be described as ordinary. Maybe the girl had been a vegetarian. She must remember to ask Nick for her name, just to make sure she never used her.

'Is this your room, Nick?' Still leaning back against the door, Cassie heard the thumb latch rattle and felt a firm shove as it was pushed from the other side. She quickly stepped to one side so that when it was opened she would be hidden behind it. 'Oh, yes.' Veronica, unexpectedly, seemed to be finding it hard to smother a giggle.

'As I said, the whole house needs decorating.'

'Actually I rather like black sheets.' Veronica began to advance into the bedroom. 'They're so wonderfully obvious. You know exactly what's going on in the mind of a man who would choose them.'

'I didn't choose them.'

Veronica ignored this rather pained response. 'Are they satin?' She crossed to the bed and touched them. 'No. Oh, well, you can't have everything.'

'Veronica — '

Cassie could see everything through the crack between the door and the architrave. Veronica was standing beside the bed and now she turned and smiled at Nick, lowering dark glossy lashes that appeared to have been individually coated with at least three coats of mascara. Then she slid her hand beneath her hair and lifted it seductively from her neck. 'I haven't thanked you yet for that lovely dinner, have I, Nick?'

'It was nothing.' *For him it had been nothing!* 'In fact — '

'You know, I've misjudged you. I'd heard all these stories about you, but you're not a bit the way Lucy described you.'

'Lucy?'

'My secretary. She warned me about you. Told me that the male staff members were laying bets about how fast you could get me into bed.'

'Really?' He cleared his throat. 'And you believed that?'

'Isn't it true?' Veronica looked positively coy. 'How disappointing.'

Cassie had to bite her lip as Nick fielded a jaw that practically hit the floor. 'Well . . . You know how it is.'

'Oh, I do, Nick. Get half a dozen men together and they just can't seem to help behaving like a bunch of schoolboys behind the bike shed.'

'They don't mean any harm.'

'That would make an admirable epitaph for the entire male sex,' she remarked dryly.

'You did invite yourself here, Veronica. And you were the one who wanted to . . . look around.'

'Well, flirting in the office is so very tacky, don't you think?'

Not half as tacky as standing behind a door listening to a man being given the green light in his own bedroom, Cassie thought. She had to do something, warn Nick that she was there before things went any further. But what? He wasn't looking her way so she could do nothing to attract his attention without Veronica seeing her too. All she could think of was to scrape gently at the back of the door with her thumb nail in an attempt to attract his attention.

'What was that?' Veronica spun round.

'Mice,' Nick said, without hesitation, and Cassie knew he'd got the message. But it was the wrong answer. With a little squeal of horror Veronica flung herself into his arms. For a moment Cassie considered leaving him to wriggle out of the situation on his own. After all, it was exactly what he had planned.

Well, not *exactly*. He hadn't *planned* on an audience.

Unfortunately the second the door closed she would be revealed, with her flushed cheeks and her totally uncontrollable hair and lashes that hadn't seen mascara in weeks. Nick would see them together and compare. He wouldn't be human if he didn't. And even if it didn't matter one jot she refused to compete with the elegant, exquisitely groomed Veronica Grant. Even if she was a wimp when it came to rodents. And Cassie wasn't convinced about that. A mouse was as good an excuse as any to fling your arms about a man.

Cassie didn't know why Nick had kissed her in the kitchen, probably simple gratitude for making his day, but she wasn't kidding herself; once he'd seen the pair of them in the same room he'd never kiss her again. Which was what she wanted, wasn't it? So why was she hesitating?

Well, there was Veronica to consider. The poor woman would be mortified if she knew she had been overheard flinging herself at a man after inveigling herself into his bedroom. *Oh, right*, her subconscious mocked, putting its hands on its hips, poking its nose in where it wasn't wanted. *And just what are you doing in his bedroom, Cassie Cornwell?*

Good grief, it wasn't as if she had planned it. It was the last place she wanted to be. And in desperation she scratched at the door again, harder this time. 'It could be rats,' Nick improvised. 'I'm getting in the pest people while I'm away . . . ' Veronica shuddered and clung even tighter, her head on his shoulder, her arms about his neck. Cassie discovered that her teeth were clenched in a totally unladylike manner and her nails, short and unpolished though they were, were digging into the palms of her hands.

'I know,' Nick said sympathetically. 'I guess it's just one of those things you have to put up with when you have a thatched roof. And the beetles are a nightmare. They keep falling into the bath. I don't suppose you know what a death-watch beetle looks like, do you? I keep hearing this tapping noise . . . ' Cassie obligingly tapped. 'Look, shall we go downstairs and I'll get you a brandy or — ?' The front doorbell rang. 'Oh, too late,' he said, with every evidence of genuine regret. 'That'll be your taxi.'

Veronica frowned. To Cassie's intense satisfaction she discovered that the woman's forehead creased just like ordinary folks'. 'Taxi? I didn't order a taxi.'

'I know, but I forgot to warn you that

it's a real problem getting one out here late in the evening, so I booked one for you.' He lied so *easily*, Cassie thought. She must remember that. 'I'd drive you myself, but I've had a glass of wine.' He eased her out of his arms and turned her towards the door. 'It's been a lovely evening, Veronica. So kind of you to risk my cooking. I'm a bit of a new hand at it . . . you must have guessed.'

'You did seem a little harassed,' she agreed. Cassie thought she might stamp her foot. Except that she'd probably fall over. 'Considering you had such expert help.'

'Help?'

Veronica walked across to the bedroom door and closed it, exposing Cassie, who, although she had pinned herself as flat as she could against the wall, was still extremely noticeable. It was probably her flushed cheeks against all that pale grey paint. 'I'm one of your biggest fans, Miss Cornwell; it was a privilege to eat something cooked personally by you. Unfortunately you're not quite as quick on your feet as you are with a whisk.'

'You saw me?'

'Twice. Once when you were diving for cover in the pantry. And a few minutes ago, making a dash for the stairs.'

There was clearly no point in denying it, so Cassie gave what she hoped was a careless shrug. 'I've sprained my ankle,' she said. 'It slowed me down.'

Veronica turned to Nick and tutted. 'Shame on you, Nick, putting this poor lady to such trouble when she's in pain.'

A sudden suspicion jagged at Cassie. 'Did you know I was in here all the time?' she asked.

Veronica gave an elegant little shrug. 'Well, there was something holding the door closed the first time I pushed it. And not the second time. Of course,' she went on, and smiled with genuine amusement, 'it could have been the combined efforts of the mice, the rats and the death-watch beetles . . . ' She clearly didn't think so.

So, the siren act had been nothing but a floor show for her benefit. And to tease Nick a little. Or perhaps a lot. Just how far would she have taken it if the doorbell hadn't rung just then? Cassie decided that she could get to like Veronica Grant, despite her height and her beanpole figure. The doorbell rang again. 'Actually, that's *my* taxi,' Cassie intervened. 'Nick was right. They do take an age out here. If you'll excuse me?'

'Would you mind very much if I took it?' Veronica asked, moving towards the door. 'Dinner was lovely, but I really think it's time I was leaving.' She extended her hand to Cassie. 'I didn't realise you still did private catering, Miss Cornwell. I was thinking of having a few colleagues round myself, just a small party but I'm hopeless in the kitchen. I'd like to think I can count on you to help me out?' She didn't wait for an answer but turned to Nick. 'Well, Nick. Thank you. I can't remember the last time I had such an entertaining evening.' She tapped him lightly on the cheek. 'I particularly enjoyed the death-watch beetle. Such good sound effects.' And with a slow wink at Cassie she left the room.

Nick, after throwing her a desperate glance, dashed after Veronica while Cassie, scarcely able to contain her laughter, collapsed on the bed in a heap and buried her face in the black duvet.

★　★　★

'Veronica!'

He found her in the mud room where she was putting on her shoes. She straightened. 'Sorry about the washing-up, Nick,' she said, with a smile as she walked out through the kitchen, the kind of smile a cat wore when he noticed that the door of the birdcage had been left open.

'I'm the one who must apologise. And I am sorry. It was a stupid thing to do.'

'But predictable.' She found her handbag in the dining room and turned to him. 'I ran a little book of my own and do you know there wasn't a single woman in the typing pool willing to risk her money on the chance that you might be telling the truth? Tell me, Nick, is Miss Cornwell reasonable?'

'Veronica . . . please . . . Cassie didn't want to do this; she just did it to help me out because . . . well, it really is too complicated to explain. But you must know that she isn't . . . she doesn't . . . '

'I do,' she said. 'But I'm sure you'll think of some way to persuade her to do the food for my party. I mean, you wouldn't want me to tell all those women that they were right about you?'

There was a third long peal on the bell. 'Frankly, Veronica, as far as I'm concerned you can tell the entire company exactly what happened — write a report and stick it on the notice board if you like.' He opened the front door for her. 'It's no more than I deserve for being such an idiot. But this isn't

Cassie's fault so I'm afraid you'll have to look for another caterer for your party.' He handed the taxi driver a ten-pound note, opened the car door and waited for her to get in. He wasn't being politically incorrect. He just wanted her to go so he could straighten things out with Cassie. Tell her that he never intended . . . at least . . .

But Veronica Grant didn't seem to be in any hurry to go. Instead she put her head on one side and regarded him for a moment. 'You're right, Nick, you are an idiot.' Then she leaned forward and kissed his cheek. 'Now hadn't you better get back inside and tell that woman exactly how you feel about her?'

★   ★   ★

'Cassie?' He was standing in the bedroom doorway, looking at her as she struggled to sit up, wiping her eyes. 'Why are you still here?'

'I'm sorry, Nick.' She had to fight hard to stifle another fit of the giggles.

232

'Truly. That must have been . . . ' She waved a hand as she struggled for some word descriptive enough.

'Embarrassing?' Nick offered.

'Disappointing. After you'd gone to so much trouble.'

'Was it deliberate?' *Deliberate?* Cassie frowned. 'The sabotage,' he elaborated.

Cassie blushed furiously. 'Of course not. Why would I want to sabotage your evening when I've gone to so much trouble to help?' He didn't bother to offer any suggestions, for which she was supremely grateful, although why she should be when he'd been doing all the kissing . . . 'It was just that I couldn't open the back door and then she decided to use the loo in the mud room and then . . . well, there was nowhere else to go but up . . . ' Nick still didn't say anything. 'Besides, she'd already seen me. Was she very angry?'

'Amused rather than angry, I think.'

'I'm sorry.'

'Don't be. It wasn't your fault. I should never have let things get this far.'

'And I shouldn't have agreed to go along with the deception.'

'You had your arm twisted.'

Not very hard. 'Will it be awkward for you?'

He thought about it for a moment. 'No, I don't think so.' Thus spoke a man with years of experience in twisting women around his little finger. It was a sobering thought. 'She did try to put a little pressure on me to get you to do some catering for her — '

'Oh, no — '

'That's more or less what I said. Don't worry about it.'

'I won't,' she declared. Then she said, 'I'd better go and call myself another taxi.'

'Don't worry, I actually did order one for Veronica.' He loosened his tie and sat down on the edge of the bed. 'Relax, Cassie. Take the weight off your feet,' he said as she began to move. 'It'll be at least twenty minutes.' Taking his own advice, he turned and stretched his length beside her. He weighed a lot more than she did and the bed dipped, tipping her towards him.

There was a moment of confusion as Cassie's body collided with his, her soft curves moulding themselves against him, her sweet-scented hair brushing his cheek and neck. He hadn't been thinking of this when he'd flopped down beside her. Or was he fooling himself?

He had been eager to get rid of Veronica but he hadn't thought much beyond that. Despite her advice, he knew he needed to think before he told Cassie anything. But as she began to struggle against the natural dip of the bed he realised this was exactly what he wanted and he wasn't about to let her run away.

'Relax, Cassie,' he repeated, slipping his arm around her. She made another move to pull free but he caught her wrist and held her. 'I have to talk to you.'

'Talk?' *Talk!* She would have laughed out loud but the warm touch of Nick's skin against her wrist had been like a jolt of electricity, driving a power surge of longing through her body. There was no time to talk; she had to move while the defence mechanisms that she had built up over the years were still functioning.

'Just talk,' he assured her. 'Trust me, Cassie.'

Trust him? On a bed, a great big double bed, covered in those obvious black sheets?

'Not in a million years,' she said. But that wasn't the problem, he wasn't the kind of man who would jump on a girl's bones when she was saying no. Although two setbacks in one night wouldn't do his self-esteem much good. Not that she was worrying about that. No, she could handle Nick Jefferson. It was herself she didn't trust.

She'd just drunk from an unexpectedly deep well of jealousy. She hadn't deliberately sabotaged Nick's evening, but honesty compelled her to admit that she would have liked to — and it hadn't been anything to do with disapproval at his cynical pretence. The realisation made her feel very vulnerable.

She hadn't been in the least bit tempted by any of the very nice men who had asked her out during the last few years. Any one of whom might have been a swan. Oh, no, not her. She had to go and fall in lust with a cuckoo like Nick Jefferson.

And now his arm was around her and she was lying with her head against his shoulder and his hand was no longer grasping her wrist; instead he was stroking the pale, sensitive skin above the heel of her hand very gently with the broad, flat tip of his thumb. She had to stop him, get away. But knowing it and doing it were two very different things.

It seemed for ever since she had been held by a man, had actually wanted to be held by a man in the sweet prelude to love. Now, lying against Nick, her cheek tucked up tight against his ribs so that she could hear his heart beating, felt like . . . like coming home.

Startled by the thought, she lifted her head to look at him. His expression echoed her own bafflement as her gaze collided with his and he stopped stroking her wrist. She heard a tiny mew of disappointment — had that been her voice? — before he quite suddenly smiled and, lifting her hand to his lips, began trailing soft, warm kisses to her elbow. It was scary and yet blissful all at the same time. Her skin was goosebumps, her insides marshmallow, her body singing as it responded to his touch. Common sense was demanding that she move. Now. Before it was too late. But then what did common sense know about need, about desire, about love?

Nick removed his arm from beneath her, pulling down a pillow and tucking it beneath her head, and Cassie lay back, her breath coming in tiny little gasps as he eased himself up onto one elbow to stare down at her, touching her cheek with the back of his fingers, stroking it thoughtfully. She shivered and licked lips dry with sudden nerves. It was years . . . it was madness . . . Her tongue bathed her lips once more and she closed her eyes.

Nothing happened and after a moment she opened them again, feeling rather foolish. That was when he kissed her. And this time it was not the delicate tasting of her lips like that first kiss in the bookshop, nor was it the swift, hard raid of his mouth when he had kissed her in the kitchen.

This was the real thing, hot and liquid, an adult kiss that went straight to the point without pretence, a kiss that left no holds barred, releasing a flood of desire to heat her skin and envelop her body in soft, dangerous excitement that stole away her will and compelled her to surrender. And when he stopped, drew back to look down at her, her head was spinning, her heart pounding, every part of her tingling with a heady mixture of fear and elation.

He must have seen all that in her face because he kissed her again, lightly, tenderly, murmuring gentle reassurance as he flipped open the top button of her shirt. Her head fell back in invitation and he placed a warm, moist kiss in the hollow of her throat, then let his mouth follow his hand as it continued its depredations of her buttons, trailing kisses down between her breasts, over her stomach, halted only by the close-fitting waistband of her jeans. She gave a little gasp as he flipped that too and let his tongue curl around her navel.

'I want you, Cassie.' Nick's words were uncompromising. He wanted her. Or more precisely, he wanted her body. No dressing it up with romantic frills. *I want you.* And whatever a Jefferson wanted he got. Win or die in the attempt. Was that all she was? Another challenge? Veronica had got away but what the heck? Cassie was still here, still hanging around his bedroom, waiting to be crossed off his wish list.

The gooseflesh suddenly returned, but this time not because of trembling, shivery passion. Then, as Nick slid his hand beneath the waistband of her jeans, he said something else. 'I think I'm falling in love with you . . . '

'Oh, no . . . '

'Want' she could believe. It had the hard stamp of honesty about it. 'Love' was something else, an easy word to use when all else failed. And he lied so easily. Cassie, her senses momentarily drugged by his kisses, was suddenly, painfully clear-headed. Without waiting for second thoughts, more lies, she put her hands on Nick's chest and pushed hard, rolling away off the bed, and while he was still trying to work out what had suddenly gone wrong she beat it to the door, ignoring the pain scything through her ankle and clutching her drooping jeans as she ran.

The main stairs, she discovered, were just a few yards further on. If only she had made them earlier none of this would have happened. Veronica might have known that Nick had tried to pull the wool over her eyes, but without a mouse behind the door to spoil the fun she might have decided to forgive him.

Damn, damn, damn. She fastened the button of her jeans as she slithered down the thick carpet of the main stairs, heading for the kitchen and the telephone.

'What on earth was that all about?' Nick demanded as she punched in the number.

She swung round, hand outstretched, daring him to come any nearer. Then, realising that her blouse was still hanging open, she grabbed the front of that instead. ''Trust me.' That's what you said, Nick. And then . . . How *could* you? Not half an hour ago you were planning to share that bed with Veronica — '

'Actually I wasn't — '

' — but she saw right through you. Well, me too. A bit late in the day perhaps, but then I'm short on that kind of experience. Although what little

242

I've had should have put me on my guard.'

'Really?' Nick's eyes glinted dangerously. 'And just what are you accusing me of, Cassie?'

'You didn't call a taxi, did you, Nick? Veronica might have walked out on you but you still had me, so there was no need to change your plans for the evening . . . ' Her voice ground to a halt as he made a move towards her, her throat drying.

'Have you quite finished?'

'No!' Then she said, less vehemently, 'Yes.' What more was there to say? Then she frowned as a voice in her ear vied for attention.

'This is Melchester Taxis; can I help you?' Something about his tone suggested it was not the first time the man had said this.

'What? Oh, yes, please. Can you send a taxi to Avonlea Cottage in Little Wickham?'

'Avonlea Cottage? Hold on.' There was a moment while Nick and Cassie continued to glare at one another. 'We despatched a taxi to that address about ten minutes ago; it should be with you any time.'

'No, that's already left — ' Her voice died as the doorbell rang. Very slowly, she turned, and through the kitchen window saw a bright 'TAXI' sign lit up on top of a car standing outside the front door. 'Oh.'

'Madam?'

Cassie shook her head, unable to speak, and Nick took the receiver from her limp fingers, apologised for the confusion and hung up.

'Now, what were you saying, Cassie?' he enquired softly. And, completely ignoring the man at the door, he leaned back against the refrigerator, folded his arms and regarded her in a manner that suggested nothing else was going to happen until he had had an explanation.

But what could she say? Sorry? I'm not very good at relationships which is why I do my best to avoid them?

Somehow she didn't think he'd want to listen to the sad and sorry tale of her failure in that department even if she'd been prepared to tell him about it. Instead, she slowly and carefully buttoned the front of her blouse.

'I think I'd better go,' she said. 'Goodbye, Nick.'

She was halfway across the kitchen before Nick spoke. 'Haven't you forgotten something, Cassie?' She picked up her basket. 'I was thinking of your shoes,' he said.

He was laughing. Damn it, he was laughing at her. Well, he could laugh all he liked; she wasn't sticking around to be the butt of his humour one more minute.

'Hang them on the wall as a reminder of the one that got away,' she said, without turning round. And she didn't stop walking until she reached the taxi.

She half expected Nick to follow her with her footwear, but he didn't. She'd banged the door of the cottage shut behind her and it stayed that way. Apparently he'd got the message.

'College Close,' she instructed the driver as he pulled away from the cottage. And she only looked back once.

Nick didn't see that. He was too busy making the first of several telephone calls.

10

Cassie didn't get much sleep that night, but then she hadn't expected to. Instead she spent the long hours checking that she had everything she might possibly need, then repacking it. Then checking it again. Anything to stop herself from thinking about what had happened. And when she'd stopped doing that she started worrying.

That helter-skelter flight down Nick's stairs hadn't done her ankle any good at all and she didn't need to be a clairvoyant to predict that she'd blown any possibility of the services of a driver and tent-erecter, even if she could have accepted them.

But those problems were nothing to the memory of how she had responded to Nick. It had been so swift, her desire so overwhelming. If only he hadn't pretended, lied. Another minute and she would have been past caring, beyond the reach of that nagging little voice that told you when you were making a complete fool of yourself.

She'd promised herself that she would never again allow her heart to rule her head. All that had died with Jonathan. And because she wasn't emotionally built for casual sex she allowed her family and friends to believe a part of her had died with him. Well, in a way it had. The part that could take a man at his word, believe him when he looked into her eyes and promised her the earth. Only a complete fool would fall for that a second time.

So she'd thrown herself into her career and hard work combined with a lot of luck had taken her to the top. She loved it. And until today it had been enough. But today she had wanted Nick, wanted him enough to throw all those years of caution to the wind. And it didn't make any sense at all. Just because she'd got it wrong about the taxi that didn't change the facts. A girl in the hand was worth any number of unavailable blondes and Nick Jefferson wasn't to be trusted further than she could throw a sack of flour.

Unfortunately, knowing that didn't make the slightest difference to the way she felt. Hormones had no sense and hers had been kept on a short lead for a long time. Now they had been so unexpectedly reminded that their proper function was to make a thorough nuisance of themselves, they were off like some stupid, adolescent Labrador who had just been given a taste of freedom, playful and eager for fun and absolutely refusing to come to heel.

She got up the moment the sky began to shimmer with a pre-dawn glow. Going to bed had been one of those automatic things, something you did even when you knew it was going to be a waste of time on the off-chance that you might be proved wrong, and Cassie was grateful to the sun for rising so early to put her out of her misery.

She made a pot of coffee, took it out into her little courtyard and watched the day begin. Dem joined her, curling up on the other chair, making it seem less empty.

She reached out to rub one of his slightly ragged ears, but for once Dem's soft purr failed to work its magic. As a cat he was the best. He might just be a saggy old mog, but he was the keeper of her secrets, a friend who would never let her down.

He was, however, still a cat and his conversation was limited to a range of purrs that started just above inaudible and rose to something resembling a Harley under full throttle when he caught a whiff of smoked salmon. Until this week, it had seemed enough. But suddenly her tall, beautiful house seemed very quiet and horribly empty.

Not that that would last for long. Matt would be along in an hour or so with the children and she'd better be ready for them. A hot shower would help — heaven alone knew when she'd get another — and a proper breakfast. Scrambled eggs, bacon, toast and a raid on the store of marmalade she had made for Christmas presents. Then she looked at the table and pulled a face. Who did she think she was kidding? A proper breakfast? This was comfort food. And she needed every mouthful.

★   ★   ★

Matt's arrival with the boys lifted her spirits a little, but her brother-in-law seemed to sense that something was wrong and assumed that it was cold feet. As they gathered on the step so that the boys could say goodbye, and despite the fact that she was making a valiant attempt not to limp, he was staring down at the strapping around her ankle with a frown.

'Are you *sure* you'll be able to manage?' he asked, for the fifth time in less than a minute. She was just about to reassure him, yet again, that she would do just fine, when they both turned to stare at a minibus reversing up the Close.

The cathedral Close was definitely not a minibus kind of place. Particularly not at seven-thirty in the morning, and Cassie knew that Nick, despite everything, had come through for her. Her heart gave a little lift at proof of his generous spirit.

As it came to a halt outside her house and Nick himself turned to look out of the driver's window, the lift became a lurch. Last night she had been convinced that she didn't want to see him, ever again. But being face to face with him put her right about that piece of self-delusion. It had been the thought of *not* seeing him ever again that had been making her so miserable. Was that better? she asked herself. Or worse? Whatever it was, she was hard-pressed to contain a grin of Cheshire cat proportions.

'Everyone ready?' he asked briskly, opening the door and jumping out so that, but for the briefest of moments when the minibus had come to a halt, he did not have to look at her. The urgent need to grin evaporated.

Worse. It was far worse. He didn't want to be here; he was just being noble.

'Isn't that Nick Jefferson?' Matt murmured. 'I didn't know that you and he . . . ' If Cassie's heart had not already been in her boots it would have sunk to them. Even without looking she knew that Matt had a great big 'what's going on here, then?' grin on his face.

'We're not,' she said, without any confidence that he would believe her.

'Does Lauren know?'

She was right. 'Of course not . . . ' Then, 'You know him?' she asked, startled into looking around, and she was right about the grin, too; her brother-in-law was grinning from ear to ear.

'I've met him at the occasional business dinner,' he said, then chuckled. 'You sly old thing, Cass. No wonder you couldn't wait to get rid of me. Just wait until I tell Lauren . . . '

About to deny that there was anything to tell, she decided that it was a waste of time. Matt wouldn't believe it . . . and there was nothing like a little sensational gossip to jump-start the conversation. They might even get around to remembering how it had been for them. How it could be again if they gave it the chance. She crossed the pavement. 'What on earth are you doing here?' she demanded, in a fierce whisper.

Nick shrugged. 'You've got three boys to take care of and since, in the absence of grandmotherly support, I've got my sister's girls I thought it might be a good idea to combine our efforts?'

'Girls?' Cassie looked past him and realised that she was being solemnly regarded by four pairs of luminous grey eyes, each pair framed by a straight fringe and neat bob of fair, shiny hair. His sister's children.

'Sadie, Bethan, Emily and Alice,' he said, introducing them. 'Say hello to Cassie, girls.'

'Hello, Cassie,' they chorused shyly.

Cassie thought her heart might melt, they were so lovely. But quite what Mike, Joe and little George would make of them — more importantly how they would feel about sharing their holiday with something as yucky as *girls* — was something else.

'Stay there, ladies, while we load up,' Nick said, giving the girls his killer smile, something he had obviously decided was wasted on her, Cassie thought. And who could blame him? Taking her consent to his high-handed plan for granted, he crossed to Matt and stuck out his hand. 'It's Matt Crosbie, isn't it? I thought I recognised you.'

He looked down at the boys. They hadn't seen the girls yet, Cassie realised, and the two youngest were looking up at Nick with something approaching awe. Mike, who seemed to understand what this trip was all about, was ignoring his father and not being exactly friendly towards her. He was wearing that bored expression that suggested nothing could impress him, not even a real live Jefferson.

Four little girls might seriously dent that laid-back, couldn't-care-less attitude if they put their minds to it, she decided, and after all found herself having to suppress a smile.

'Mike, Joe and George,' Cassie filled in brightly. 'This is Mr Jefferson, boys.'

'That's a bit formal; why don't you just call me Nick?' he invited. 'I hope you don't mind a bit of company on your trip but I thought your aunt could do with a hand this week.' The little ones beamed. Mike, on the other hand, found something excessively interesting about the toes of his trainers. 'Maybe you could start by carrying these things out to the van for her?' Nick prompted.

Ignoring Cassie's urgent shake of the head, Nick opened up the rear of the van for them and Joe and little George almost fell over themselves to co-operate. Mike remained slouched against the doorpost.

'Can you bring that box, Mike?' Nick asked, pointing to a large carton of groceries that Joe was struggling to pick up. 'It's too heavy for Joe.' Mike glared at his father, glared at Cassie, then pushed his brother aside and picked up the box and carried it across to Nick. He didn't take it. 'There's plenty of room in there,' he said, leaving the boy to deal with it himself. 'You'll make sure everything's stowed properly, won't you?' he added as George staggered up with a small box. 'Don't bother to bring all that camping gear, Joe. I've got everything we'll need.' Then he rejoined Matt who was watching the procession of goods disappearing into the van with a touch of anxiety.

'I hope there's nothing breakable in those boxes.'

'Eggs,' Cassie offered.

'If the boys break them they won't have any for breakfast,' Nick said matter-of-factly as Mike practically threw the box into the van. 'And since you don't eat more than organic yoghurt and a banana for breakfast it's hardly going to worry you, is it?' Cassie's cheeks heated up under Matt's amused scrutiny and she wanted to explain that Nick only knew what she had for breakfast because she'd told him. But since she knew she would be wasting her breath she didn't bother. 'Cassie tells me you're off to Portugal, Matt.'

'Just a short break . . . Look, this is very good of you, Nick. To be honest Lauren was a bit concerned about Cass going off on her own and now with her ankle . . . '

'Exactly my own thoughts.'

'Will you please not talk about me as if I'm not here?' Cassie asked.

'If it offends you,' Nick suggested, his voice teasing for Matt's benefit, his eyes not making the same effort, 'why don't you make a final tour of the house and make sure everything is locked up? Anyone could climb over that back wall and break in.'

She glared at him. 'Not when I've got the alarm switched on, they couldn't.

And if they tried our extremely vigilant neighbourhood watch would soon sort them out.' What a pity they didn't sell burglar alarms for the heart. Still, until this week she'd have sworn she didn't need one. And now it was too late. She gave Matt a hug and a little push. 'Go. You'll miss your plane. Give my love to Lauren. And give her yours, too,' she added meaningfully.

'Yes, I'd better be going. Here, I won't be needing these.' And, hanging onto his own car keys, he handed back the keys to Cassie's little sports car.

'Oh, but — '

Matt glanced at the minibus with a grin. 'You won't be needing the estate now, will you?'

I do, she thought. *I do!* But Matt was already striding across the pavement, a lot happier about leaving the boys with her now that he thought she had company. And she could always rent a car. Or even go along with Nick's crazy plan. There was no reason not to since it was clear he'd lost all interest in making passes at her; his only interest was in making her feel bad. Not that he needed to do that; she felt quite bad enough already.

'Goodbye, boys. And do *try* and behave,' Matt said, ruffling their hair as he climbed back into the big Mercedes estate that she had been going to borrow for the trip. Mike ducked to avoid his hand.

'Have a good time,' she called, encouraging the boys to wave as he drove off, putting off for as long as possible the moment when she would have to turn and face Nick.

But he had already moved away and was checking the boys had loaded the minibus properly. He'd come to help her out as he'd promised, but he wasn't going to pretend he liked it. So she went inside, not to check the windows and doors, but so that she wouldn't have to watch the way the low sun was filtering through his hair as he pushed it back off his forehead; so that she didn't have to notice the way the collar of his polo shirt curved away from his neck, the way it clung invitingly to his back to display the powerful paired muscles.

'Ready?' Cassie had been staring out of the French windows, trying to decide what was the best thing to do, and she jumped as he came up behind her. 'You should take something for those nerves,' he said.

'There's nothing wrong with my nerves. I was thinking, that's all.'

'Oh? I'd give a penny for those thoughts.'

'Don't be cheap, Nick. They're worth at least a pound if you take inflation into account.'

'You strike a hard bargain, but go on, surprise me.'

'There won't be enough food for all of us,' she said briskly, gathering herself, relying on practicalities to save her.

'I dare say I can manage a trip to a supermarket,' he said. 'I'm beginning to get the hang of them.'

'You've never tried it with seven children in tow.'

'We could rope them together — '

'You don't have to do this, Nick.' She turned and looked up at him, desperate for him to understand. But how could he, when he didn't know? 'It's kind,' she rushed on, before he could say anything. 'More than kind, after the way I behaved last night — '

'The least said about last night the better.' He reached out as if about to touch her arm, then apparently thought better of it as she flinched away from him. 'We made a deal,' he said abruptly. 'You kept your part of the bargain, I'm here to keep mine.'

'But last night . . . last night was not a success.'

'That was my fault, Cassie, not yours.'

Beth had asked him when he was going to grow up. Now he knew. He just hoped it wasn't too late. He'd grown up during an apparently endless night when the only thing on his mind was how to convince Cassie that he loved her. When, last night, he had said it, he had been just as shaken as she had been. But it was inevitable, after that stupid stunt with Veronica, that she had thought he was simply stringing her a line to get her into bed.

'I should never have agreed to have anything to do with such a stupid trick,' she said.

'I should never have asked you,' he replied evenly.

'I suppose you've sent Veronica a big bunch of flowers by way of damage limitation?'

'Flowers are just a bit too easy, a bit too glib, don't *you think?*'

'I suppose they are rather obvious,' she agreed. And he never did anything obvious. 'What did you do?'

'Actually I called her late last night and told her that my uncle had agreed to offer her a seat on the board if she'd join us permanently.'

Something froze, deep inside. 'I guess some mistakes are so big that they need the really grand gesture.' And Nick had told her himself that a Jefferson refused to consider defeat. 'Did it do the trick?'

she managed to ask, even managed to sound as if it didn't matter. But then she was good at hiding her feelings. She'd had a lot of practice.

'She didn't exactly fall over herself to accept,' he said, somewhat wryly. 'She's thinking about it.'

'*Thinking* about it?' Was the woman *mad*?

'She runs her own consultancy at the moment. It's a lot to give up, but she'd be quite a catch.'

'Yes, I could see last night that she would be.'

'Can we get back to the more immediate problem, Cassie? If I don't help out with the camping trip how will you manage?'

'Actually, since you mention it, that is a bigger problem than I had anticipated.' She risked a look at him. He didn't look quite himself this morning either. A bit crumpled around the eyes as if he hadn't slept much. That surprised her. Surely even Nick Jefferson failed to score occasionally? And he still had the lovely Veronica to tempt with a directorship. *Stop it, Cass! You said no. Forget it*. She forced herself to concentrate on the matter in hand. 'Matt was supposed to take the Alfa and leave the estate with me,' she explained. 'But that's not your problem.'

'No? I think you're saying that when he saw me arrive with the minibus he jumped to the very obvious conclusion that you wouldn't be needing it.' He didn't say that she could easily have disabused Matt of that impression, she noticed, which was tactful of him. She wasn't sure she liked him tactful. She preferred him forthright, rude even, because that at least meant he was feeling something. Polite and tactful were just so . . . cold. 'How about this, Cassie? Suppose I give you and the boys a lift to where you're going as I promised — '

'You promised me an eager young man to drive and put up the tent,' she reminded him.

'I might be past thirty but I think I

can still handle a tent, Cassie.'

'Yes, but — '

Apparently 'buts' were not to be entertained. 'If the girls like it there, we can stay too. On the other side of the field if it makes you happier.'

'They'll hate it.'

'Then you've nothing to worry about, have you?' Dem, squeezing his bulk in through the catflap, gave Nick a sardonic look. 'If they don't like it I'll bring them home and come back and fetch you whenever you want.'

Put like that there really could be no objection. The alternative was to hire a car and drive them herself. But that would take all morning and they wouldn't arrive at Morgan's Landing until late, when she'd have to put up a couple of tents, light a fire, get supper . . . And there was still the problem of her ankle.

Of course they could stay at home and she could take them out on day trips — one of her midnight solutions — but when they'd been promised camping in the wilds day trips would come a very poor second best. And Mike was already looking decidedly sullen. He had been putting on a couldn't-care-less face for his father, but he cared. He was old enough to understand what was happening and he was scared enough to take it out on any adult within range. It would be a relief to share that burden.

Mike chose that moment to explode into the kitchen. 'There are *girls* in that minibus! Four of them!' he declared, in disgust.

Nick turned a sympathetic look on him. 'Approximately fifty per cent of the world's population are female, Mike. You might as well get used to it.'

Mike glared at him. 'Do we *have* to go with them, Cassie?'

'Well, I suppose we could stay here for the week,' she offered. 'Take a few bus trips.'

'Bus trips!'

His horrified expression clinched it and she lifted one trouser leg an inch or two to display her strapping. 'I sprained my ankle, Mike, so driving is a bit of a problem. I didn't want to spoil your parents' holiday by telling them how much of one. I don't think you do either.' She waited.

'No, I suppose not,' he said, capitulating with bad grace, but apparently prepared to accept the lesser of two evils.

'Then let's go.'

★ ★ ★

For the first part of the journey the boys kept to one side of the minibus and the girls kept to the other. Nick and Cassie kept conversation to a minimum too.

But by the time they had stopped for elevenses the ice had cracked sufficiently for the younger children to be making as much noise as a Women's Institute outing. Only Mike was still doing the strong, silent thing, a personal stereo clamped firmly to his head. And Sadie hadn't taken her big grey eyes off him since he'd climbed aboard the bus. Cassie suspected an embryonic case of hero worship and hoped it would soothe Mike's feelings a little. Take his mind off adult worries.

Nick noticed the smile as Cassie turned back to face the front and he felt like smiling too. He'd been wondering what it would take to bribe four girls to spend a week in a field without running water, but it didn't look as if bribery was going to be necessary after all. The younger children were getting on like a house on fire and he recognised the look on Sadie's face. She wasn't about to let Mike out of her sight.

He wasn't kidding himself that Cassie was going to be such a pushover. Last night, after he'd rung Graham to tell him his plan for looking after the girls while he and Helen were away, he'd rung Beth and he'd put his heart on the line.

'In love? You're kidding.' She'd laughed. He didn't blame her.

'I wish I was.'

'Who's the unlucky girl?'

'Cassie Cornwell.' There had been no more laughter, only an ominous silence. 'Beth, please. I've made a complete mess of this and I need to know — '

'What?' She sounded cagey.

'Anything. Anything that will help me. Tell me about her husband. What happened?'

'If Cassie doesn't want to tell you — '

'Beth!'

'She's emotionally fragile, Nick. You can't treat her like one of your casual conquests . . . '

'Beth, I'm serious. I intend to marry her. But when I told her I loved her she seemed to clam up.'

'Can you blame her? Your reputation goes before you.'

'I've never lied to any woman about the way I feel, Beth. I've had a lot of fun but I've never told a woman I loved her before . . . With Cassie it just sort of happened . . . '

'Hey. You've got it bad, haven't you?'

'It's terminal. Will you help me?' He didn't wait for her agreement. 'Tell me about her husband. Did he hit her?'

'Hit her? Good grief, Nick, whatever makes you think that? Jonathan and Cassie were so in love it lifted your heart to see them. And they just couldn't wait to get married. And for Cassie and Jonathan it had to be marriage.'

'I see.'

'If her parents had still been alive it would have been the whole works, the cathedral, the bishop, but in the event they just got a licence and they were married at the register office.'

'So why didn't they live happily ever after?'

'Because three weeks later he was dead. He'd been up north somewhere to a race meeting; he was in blood stock, you see.'

'Blood stock?'

'He bought and sold racehorses.'

'Oh, yes, of course.'

'No one knows exactly what happened;

he just lost control of the car and ploughed into a motorway bridge.' Nick muttered something fierce beneath his breath. 'I thought she was going to die of grief,' Beth said. 'It was only work that kept her sane, I think . . . the fact that she refused to let people down and just kept going. And then she met this girl at my wedding who asked her to do a spot on some daytime television show, she moved to London and now she's a storming success.'

'How long ago was this?'

'Five years.'

'And there hasn't been anyone else in all that time?'

'She says she's a swan and apparently they mate for life, so if you're not serious, Nick, leave well alone,' she warned. 'Please.'

Now he glanced across at Cassie. She was staring out of the window as if absorbed by the passing scenery, but she wasn't really looking at it; she was lost in thought. He would have given anything to know what exactly was going through her mind.

'We'll be turning off the motorway soon,' he said, and she gave a little shudder as she gathered herself and turned to look at him.

There were dark smudges beneath her lovely golden eyes, which held a wary expression that tugged at something deep inside him. He wanted to stop the minibus and take her into his arms and tell her that he loved her more than life itself, that he would die for her if necessary, that he wouldn't let anything hurt her ever again. But he didn't. And it wasn't just the prospect of seven children as an audience that stopped him.

Before he could risk such a declaration he had to regain her trust. He had to show her that she could believe in him. No matter how long it took.

'Have you got that map handy?' he asked.

11

Morgan's landing was unexpectedly beautiful. Sheep-cropped grass sloped down to a small lake where a small wooden jetty stretched out into the water, with a dinghy tied up alongside. Across the water a small island seemed to shimmer in the heat of the early afternoon and around them the mountains seemed close enough to touch.

And despite her worst fears about lack of sanitation Cassie discovered that there was a small building housing a couple of showers as well as toilet facilities.

'We're lucky to have this to ourselves at this time of year,' Nick said, looking around.

'I think Matt arranged it that way. He knows the owner.'

'Oh, I see.' He nodded towards the dinghy. 'What about the boat? Can we use it?'

'Matt hired the dinghy when he thought he was going to be bringing the boys. I suppose he forgot to cancel it.'

'You don't sail?' She shook her head. 'Mike?'

'I've done a bit,' the boy said grudgingly, but his eyes, fixed hungrily on the dinghy, betrayed him. 'Dad said he'd give me some lessons.' He kicked at the grass. 'He's a really good sailor. He won cups.'

'Well, I don't suppose I can compete with that, but I'll do my best.'

'I'd like to learn, Uncle Nick,' Sadie put in, a touch too eagerly and earned herself a look of disdain from Mike.

'Me too, me too,' the smaller children shouted, clamouring excitedly around him.

'Well, that should keep us all out of Cassie's hair.' Keep *me* out of your hair if that's what you want, he offered silently as their gazes met briefly over the children's heads. *She should, but she didn't*. So it was perhaps as well that he didn't hang around for an

275

answer. 'But first things first. We've got to get this camp up and running before we can do anything else and if everyone helps it won't take long.' Within minutes the children were eagerly unloading the minibus; even Mike was joining in with some enthusiasm. Cassie was still watching Nick when he turned back to her and caught her. 'I find that carrots work better than sticks, don't you?'

'Every time. I don't know what I would have done without you today, Nick.'

'Hold onto that thought,' he said as he saw something wistful in her expression. Regret? Could it possibly be regret? Or was he just fooling himself? Maybe she was just thinking about the way it might have been for her if her husband hadn't been killed. And yet the way she had come into his arms, responded to him . . . He decided to risk a smile, anyway. 'It looks as if you're stuck with us for the duration.'

His smile was answered in the most

perfunctory way. 'I just hope you don't live to regret it.'

'Not for a . . . George! Not that one, it's too — ' he didn't make it to the van before the boy staggered back with the box containing the eggs ' — heavy,' Nick finished as it fell to the ground. The child began to cry but before Cassie could rush to comfort him one of the girls had put her arm around him, given him a hug and started to help him gather up the spilled groceries. 'Not for a minute,' Nick finished, but quietly, to himself.

*   *   *

Four days of perfect sunshine finally broke with squalls of rain at lunchtime on their last full day. The temperature dropped sharply and the lake, until now a millpond on which Nick had seemed to spend most of his time teaching even the youngest of the children the rudiments of sailing, was now an angry, churning slate-grey.

'We could pack up now,' Nick suggested as they took shelter in one of the bigger tents to drink the tinned tomato soup that Cassie had warmed through to go with their sandwiches.

'No, we can't — '

'Not until tomorrow — '

Mike and Sadie spoke as one and the little ones took up the clamour. 'The weather forecast says this rain will pass,' Sadie added, as if that settled the matter. 'I heard it on my personal stereo radio.'

'That's right,' Mike put in.

'Really?' Nick flicked a lazy grin over the two of them. 'Were you two sharing a headset?' he asked.

Mike flushed. 'Of course not!' He threw a glance at Sadie. 'She told me.'

'Cassie, what do you think?' he asked politely.

'Well, I had planned a sort of camp feast. I suppose it would be a shame to miss it.'

'Whatever you say.'

He was still being polite, Cassie

thought, and a cold spot of misery that had settled somewhere about where her heart should be seemed to chill another degree or two. Four days of politeness had brought it almost to freezing point.

Not that she could complain about anything. He'd done more, far more, than she had ever asked of him. He'd run the camp, dealt with wasps, spiders and earwigs without a murmur. He'd taken the children on wood-gathering trips and kept the fire pit blazing at night when they'd all sat out with their mugs of cocoa, even produced marsh-mallows to float in them. He'd been a perfect uncle for the boys as well as the girls. And a perfect gentleman to her.

There had been no more stolen kisses.

And the only time he had touched her had been when they had walked up to the farm for the milk and eggs. Usually Mike and Sadie did this chore, but the farm dog had had puppies and the little ones had been invited to visit and see them.

At the top of the field there was a stile. Nick had gone first and as each of the children had climbed up and over he'd caught them and swung them to the ground.

He'd taken her arm to steady her as she'd climbed up and then, as he'd held out his hands to lift her down, her ankle had given way and she had practically fallen into his arms. He'd held her for just a moment longer than had been quite necessary, his arms tight about her as she'd clung to him for support, her heart pounding, her head just a little dizzy from his closeness.

His heart, too, had seemed to be beating with a rather hectic rhythm. After endless moments she'd dared to look up and for just a moment, a breathless moment, she had thought he was going to kiss her, right there in the field with all the children looking on. Instead he'd tucked her arm beneath his and walked with her up the path to the farm. A perfect gentleman.

But ever since then she had been

reliving not only the stolen kisses, but the ones that had been freely given, fantasising about them, yearning for more. But the only indication that he might be having similar feelings had come when, unable to sleep, she had walked down to the lakeside just after dawn and seen him swimming far out in the lake, slicing through the freezing water as if some Celtic relative of the Loch Ness monster were after him.

She must have been mad to agree to stay on when she had the chance to leave. The sooner she went home to reality the better. 'What will you do this afternoon if it stays wet?' she asked, in an attempt to drive out thoughts of Nick Jefferson.

'We'll think of something,' Sadie said, giggling. 'Come on, everyone, let's go to the other tent; I've got an idea.'

'Haven't you forgotten the washing-up?' Nick reminded her.

'Let them go. It's their last day.' Cassie began to gather the mugs and plates.

'It's our last day, too. Leave those, Cassie, I want to talk to you.'

'What about?' She continued to gather the dishes busily until he put out a hand and took hold of one of hers, stopping her. She looked up. His face was intent, almost desperate. 'What is it, Nick?'

'Beth told me. About your husband.' He hadn't known what he was going to say, only that he had to say something. 'She warned me. She said if I wasn't serious I shouldn't think of getting involved with you. I have to tell you now that I've never been more serious about anything in my whole life before.'

'What about Veronica?'

'Veronica?'

'You're giving her a directorship; I would have thought that was pretty serious.'

'I didn't want her — '

'Making a fool of you?'

'Good God, I didn't care about that. When you behave like an idiot you have to take the consequences. It was your reputation I was thinking of, Cassie. The directorship was going to be offered to her anyway. I told her about it because I knew she would think twice about indulging the typing pool's love of gossip if she was going to be a permanent fixture. And when I told her about the directorship I also told her that I intended to marry you. If you'd have me.' She was staring at him, her face shuttered and barred so that he couldn't tell what she was thinking. 'Look, leave those.' He got up. 'Let's get out of here and go for a walk.'

'We can't leave the children.' She began to collect the rest of the plates, but he bent down and caught her hand. It was trembling.

'Come on,' he said, taking her other hand and drawing her to her feet. 'Just along by the lake. We'll see the children if they come anywhere near the water.'

'Nick, it's pouring with rain.' She sounded almost desperate, he thought.

'I thought we'd already agreed that a walk along the beach in the rain is the height of romance.'

Romance? 'There isn't a beach. At least not much of one.'

'Imagine it. Here, put my jacket on; it'll keep you dry.' He fed her arms into his waxed jacket as if she were a child, zipping it up to the chin, fastening the collar around her face so that little more than her eyes showed.

'What about you?'

'I'll survive.' He held back the tent flap and then took her arm and tucked it beneath his as he straightened beside her.

'I'd better just check — ' she began, shying away like a nervous colt. But shrieks of laughter were coming from the other tent and Nick kept her close. 'Oh, well. They seem happy enough.'

'They're fine.'

Neither of them spoke as they walked down to the edge of the lake, but as the waves of rain came in across the water, soaking their hair, running down their faces, Cassie stared across at the island and said, 'This is madness.'

'Probably,' Nick agreed. And they both knew they weren't talking about the weather. Then he turned to her. 'I'll wait, Cassie. As long as you like. I want you to be as sure as I am about this. But I want you to know that I'm not going away. Not unless you tell me there can't ever be any hope. And if you tell me that I shan't believe you.'

'You think you're that irresistible?' She turned on him with a show of resistance, eyes sparking for the first time in days.

'No, Cassie. You've been resisting me ever since I walked into Beth's shop and I'm sure you intend to carry on doing just that. But you're finding it a lot harder than you'd like. And, once or twice, when your guard has slipped, your real feelings have shown through. Do you want to tell me about it?'

'I'm sure Beth filled you in on all the details.'

'Beth told me what she thought was the truth. That you were love's young dream, that it ended in tragedy and your heart was irretrievably broken. I don't believe that. At least not the bit about love's young dream.' She spun round and looked up at him. And he saw fear, real fear in her eyes. 'Can you look me in the eye and tell me that I'm wrong?'

Her mouth opened, then closed and he saw something like a war going on behind her eyes. He wanted to tell her that it didn't matter. Not to him. Whatever had happened. But until she had faced the past she didn't have a future. Not a real future. Only a career.

'Cassie?' he prompted gently.

'No. You're not wrong. I thought it was, but I made a mistake.'

Because he knew it would be easier for her to talk if she didn't have to look at him, he turned with her and began to walk along the shore. 'He hit you, didn't he?'

There was a shocked silence that told him he was right. Then her deep, shuddering breath came to him over the sound of the rain. 'No, he didn't hit me,

Nick. But he would have done if Dem hadn't flown at him and clawed his arm. How did you guess?'

'Your remark about Dem not liking men very much did make me wonder why. And then, when I dumped you rather unceremoniously onto the sofa, he reacted like a little tiger.' He glanced down at her. Her head was bowed, her hair soaked through.

'He might just be a bad-tempered cat.'

'He might. But when the policeman asked you if you wanted someone from the domestic violence unit to visit you you went quite white. I think that's probably why he was so persistent.'

'You were supposed to be delivering a message to his partner, not eavesdropping!'

'I know. I gave myself a good talking-to afterwards.' He found her hand in the depths of his sleeve and she didn't reject him when he took it in his own. 'What went wrong, Cassie?'

'It was nothing complicated, or intense. No other women. Or men,' she added, in case he might have some idea that she was to blame. 'It was all about money.' He said nothing. 'Jonathan was a gambler and he married me for my money. By the time he discovered that I didn't have any that he could use to pay his debts, his ring was on my finger and he was trapped. And very angry.' She gave a convulsive little shudder and didn't pull away when he put his arms about her and held her close.

'I did wonder about the speed of the wedding.'

'His idea, of course. And I was too much in love to question his reasons.' She looked up at him. 'I've never told anyone what happened, Nick. Not even my sister.'

He glanced at a fallen log. 'Shall we sit down?' She nodded. 'I won't tell a soul, Cassie. You can trust me.'

'Can I?'

He heard the uncertainty in her voice and understood it. One man had let her down badly and he hadn't exactly proved himself the soul of probity. This wasn't the moment for an over-the-top 'with your life' declaration. 'I may not be perfect but I don't gossip. Nothing you tell me will go any further.' Her eyes still doubted him. 'I do think you should tell someone.'

She looked around him and then gave the smallest of shrugs. 'There's no one else here so I guess you're it.'

It took her a while to get started, but once she did it all came tumbling out. 'It was the house he was after. It's been in the family for generations and when my parents died in a coach crash it came to Lauren and me. Lauren was married by then, Mike was a toddler, Joe was on the way and she wanted a garden. She never did like living in the city. I was still living at home, so I paid her rent for her half and started up my catering business with my share of some compensation money we were awarded from the crash.' She sighed. 'I suppose Jonathan must have read about the compensation in the local news-paper and thought I might be easy pickings. Then he discovered I was living in this really big, very valuable house and he decided to stake everything on one throw of the dice. As I said, he was a gambler.'

'How did he meet you?'

'At one of the functions I catered. He said he was a blood-stock dealer, dropped names the way a careless cook drops cherries, and he simply oozed charm and excitement. Prince Charming couldn't have done it better. He was just too good to be true, looking back. No one is that perfect. It had to be an act.'

'He seems to have taken in everyone. What about his family?'

'Living abroad. In South Africa. We would visit them on an extended honeymoon when he wasn't so busy, he said. That at least was true. I had a lovely letter from his mother when he died, thanking me for making his last weeks happy, inviting me to visit.'

'They didn't know what he was like?'

'Maybe they did. Maybe they were

like me, just pretending.' She looked at him, her cheeks wet with rain or tears, her eyelashes clumped together, her hair clinging to her forehead. 'The first I knew that anything was wrong was when the bank manager phoned me to ask whether I wanted to extend my overdraft facility. Until that point I didn't know I had an overdraft. But he had cleaned out my account — our account; I had changed it to joint names when we were married. Of course he had a perfectly plausible excuse about covering the cost of the purchase of some horse until the new owner's cheque cleared. But when I called in at the bank to sort things out I discovered that he'd taken the deeds of the house from the bank's safe.'

'But he couldn't just sell it without you finding out.'

'He couldn't sell it at all. But he hadn't wanted to sell it, just use the deeds to cover some bookmaker's debt. That's when the pretence came to an end. I was waiting for him to come home and tax him with it, but he didn't wait for that. His bookmaker had told him that the deeds wouldn't do. He wanted his money.'

'What was the matter with them?'

'The house is held in trust for us. It would take all of us — Lauren and me *and* the trustees — to agree a sale.'

That was when Jonathan had told her the truth. That there was no job, that he gambled and that sometimes he lost. He had told her that he didn't care about her at all, that their whirlwind romance had been provoked by an urgent need for money. Or, more particularly, for her house, which he was going to use as collateral to cover an embarrassment of debt. If she didn't persuade her sister and the trustees that the house must be sold, he would go to prison.

'And you said no?'

Cassie stirred. 'It was like having a revelation. I saw him for what he was, Nick — a very nasty man inside a beautiful body — and I discovered that love at first sight has an equal and opposite emotion. Saying no was easy.'

He had changed before her eyes from Jekyll to Hyde and would have beaten her but as he'd raised his hand Dem had leapt at him, clawing at him. He'd knocked the cat halfway across the room and then he'd left. Walked out. Two days later the police had called to tell her that he had driven into the bridge superstructure on a motorway somewhere in Yorkshire.

'Suicide?'

'I don't know. The verdict was accidental death, but on the day of his funeral the deeds were dropped through the letter box in a plain brown envelope. I sometimes wonder if perhaps they'd given up on him and used him as an example . . . '

Nick said something brief and to the point under his breath. 'No wonder your friends feared for your sanity.'

'Did they?'

'Beth said that only your work kept you sane.'

'Jonathan's only legacy was a pile of debts, Nick. Gambling debts die with you, but the credit card companies don't take the same view of things. I didn't work hard to forget, I worked to keep my head above water.'

'I can see why you'd find it hard ever to trust anyone again.'

'Do you really think that's the problem? Don't you see, Nick? I thought I was head over heels in love with Jonathan. I married him, for pity's sake. But if I had really been in love with him I would have stuck by him, done anything to help him. It may not be particularly bright, but it's what women in love do. But I didn't want to stick by him. I just wanted him out of my life.'

'That's a misplaced sense of guilt.'

'Maybe it is. I didn't wish him dead, just gone, but I couldn't feel sorry . . . just relieved . . . '

'You shouldn't be so hard on yourself. He didn't think twice about destroying you and if you let him deprive you of the life you should have he's still won.'

'He's not depriving me of anything.' And it was true, she suddenly realised. 'I've been blaming him for that all this time, telling myself that I couldn't ever trust another man, but it's not true.' Her hands flew to her cheeks. 'Oh, God, how could I have been so stupid? The reason I can't, won't get involved with anyone is because if I could make such a mistake about him . . . if I could think I was so in love . . . ' She turned her face to his, a mute appeal for understanding in her eyes. 'Don't you see, Nick? I couldn't ever trust my judgement again.'

'You wouldn't make the same mistake a second time.'

'Can you be sure? Would you really want to take the risk?'

He reached out and laid his palm against her cheek. 'I'd take a risk on you right now, Cassie. But I'm not the one who needs convincing.'

'It'll never happen.'

'It will. One day. You'll know when.'
He stood up and, taking her hand,
pulled her up alongside him. 'Come on.
We'd better go and see what the kids
are up to.'

★   ★   ★

'Cassie?' She had only been asleep for
what seemed like seconds when Cassie
heard an insistent little voice in her ear.
'Cassie?' It was Bethan, she realised,
and she opened one eye. It was, as she
had feared, still pitchdark. 'Cassie, has
Sadie come back yet?'

'Sadie?' she repeated groggily. 'Has
she gone to the loo?' She was getting
braver if she'd make the dash across the
field in the dark by herself. Awake now,
Cassie sat up and groped for her torch.
'Do you want to go, sweetheart? Just let
me find my jacket.'

'Sadie hasn't gone to the loo, Cassie.
She's gone somewhere with Mike. I
heard them saying . . . '

At three o'clock in the morning

Cassie might not be at her best, but something about the child's anxious words jolted her awake faster than a cold shower. *With Mike!*

A quick flash of the torch over the sleeping bags confirmed her worst fears. Sadie was gone and so was her sleeping bag. 'Stay there, Bethan.'

She pushed open the tent flap. It wasn't exactly raining, but something wet, a cross between a drizzle and a mist, immediately clung to her face. She pushed her feet into her shoes and, the light from the torch swinging about as she ran, she dashed to the other tent, unzipped the flap and flashed the torch across the sleeping figures. Three of them. No Mike.

'Nick!' she whispered urgently.

He threw up an arm to shade his eyes as she shone the torch into his face. 'What the hell . . . ?'

'It's Mike and Sadie. They're missing.'

12

'Bethan, darling, try to think,' Nick said gently, curbing his anxiety as he quizzed the child. 'What exactly did you hear Mike say?'

'He said ... he said ... ' She yawned.

'She's asleep on her feet, Nick.'

'Bethan,' he said, with a touch more urgency. 'It's really important that you tell us what you heard.'

'I heard Mike,' the child mumbled, close to tears. 'He said he was going to run away and live on the island.' She sniffed.

'But why?'

'Because he gave his mummy a headache. And when his mummy had a headache his daddy was unhappy.'

'I should have known,' Cassie said, furious with her sister for letting things get to this point. 'He pretends to be tough but he's not.'

'And Sadie?' Nick demanded. 'Why did she go?'

'Sadie said he'd have to take her with him, or she'd tell.'

'That figures. Little madam.' Cassie and Nick exchanged a glance. 'Put her back to bed, Cassie. I'll check the boat.'

'But they couldn't have . . . It was dark . . .'

'If the boat's there, I'll come back.'

'And if it isn't?' she whispered as a deep cold feeling of dread settled in the pit of her stomach.

'I'll call the police. They can organise a search the minute it gets light.'

'Nick?'

All her fear was in that one syllable and he held her for just a moment. 'It'll be all right, sweetheart. Why don't you get the kettle going? They'll be cold . . .' He left the sentence unfinished. The temperature had dropped with the rain. They'd be cold. And if he didn't find them soon they'd stay that way.

Cassie settled Bethan back in her

sleeping bag and the little girl was asleep before she'd pulled up the zip. Then she crossed to the cook tent and, fumbling in the darkness, lit the storm lantern and put a kettle on to boil.

Deep down she knew that Nick had only asked her to do it to keep her occupied, but he was right. If he found the children they would be cold.

When he found the children, not *if*. And he would find them. They couldn't have sailed out to the island in the dark. They wouldn't be so naughty. If anything had happened to them . . .

She turned as she heard Nick behind her. 'They've taken the boat.'

'No-o-o-o . . . ' The word was a long and desperate need for it not to be so. 'They'll be so frightened,' she muttered into his chest as he held her close for a moment.

'I'll call the police now.' He held her at arm's length so that he could look at her. 'They'll be all right, Cassie. I promise you they'll be all right.'

And while he held her she believed

him. But the moment he left her to use his mobile phone all her doubts came flooding back. Her poor sister. Helen. The children. How would they cope? How would she be able to live with herself?

'Stop it,' she said, out loud, then spun around as Nick returned. 'Are they coming?'

'They'll be here at first light.'

'But that's not for hours.'

'It just seems that way, Cassie,' he said sympathetically. 'It's two at the most but they can't do anything much before then. I thought I'd drive the minibus down to the water's edge and shine the lights across the lake. We might see something. At least, if they're frightened, they'll know we're doing something.'

'But we aren't doing anything! We're standing here wringing our hands and doing absolutely nothing at all — '

'I'll get the minibus.'

'I'm coming with you.'

They bounced across the field, the

headlights illuminating first the grass, then the lake and the patches of drifting mist that clung to the still water.

'What's that?' she said, scrambling out of the van, her feet thudding hollowly against the wooden jetty as she raced along it, certain that she had seen something in the headlights.

'It's just the mist, Cassie,' Nick said, coming up behind her.

'No. I'm sure I saw a sail.'

'They won't get far with a sail; the wind's dropped right away. I'm afraid if they're heading for the island they'll have to row.' He took a step nearer the edge of the jetty, then turned back abruptly. 'Have you still got the night binoculars in your tent?'

'I think so. Why? What have you seen?'

'Nothing, probably. But I'd like a better look.'

She didn't stop to debate it, but Emily woke and had to be comforted, then the binoculars were not in her bag where she'd left them when they'd been

302

watching a badger up in the woods. After wasting valuable time hunting for them, it occurred to her that Sadie might have taken them with her. And she wondered what else they'd taken.

She couldn't see Nick on the jetty as she returned to break the news that as well as the night glasses Mike and Sadie had helped themselves to what was left of the tinned food, suggesting a certain amount of forward planning. Except for the fact that they'd overlooked the need for a tin opener. A loaf of bread was gone, too. But Mike had left something behind in its place. A note.

Nick wasn't in the van, either. She called out, swinging her torch in an arc around the lake edge, across the jetty. She sighed with relief as the light picked out something at the far end. For a moment she thought he was leaning over the edge but as she got closer she saw that it wasn't Nick at all.

For a moment she couldn't make it out. Then she knew exactly what it was. A pile of clothes. She began to run towards it, hoping against hope that she might be wrong. But she wasn't. As she picked up the thick shirt that he had hastily donned when she'd woken him, she caught the scent of woodsmoke, mingled with Nick's own special smell. A mixture of soap and shampoo and his skin; during the last few days it seemed to have seeped into her pores so that she would never forget it.

He'd gone after them. She had complained that they were doing nothing but wringing their hands, so he'd made an excuse to send her away so that he could go after them. A grand gesture, indeed.

'Nick!' Her voice cried out in the darkness like a pain, a pain that echoed and grew as it reverberated around the hills. 'Nick!' It was a cry full of desperation, but there was no answer.

He could swim, she knew that; she'd seen him slicing through the water like a porpoise. But in the dark, with the swirling mist, he could so easily lose his sense of direction, miss the island, swim around in circles until he was exhausted. And she knew he'd taken the risk for her. He knew that for her waiting until light would be like some endless nightmare. But he knew, too, that she would have tried to stop him.

Yesterday he'd told her that she would know when she could trust her feelings. Was this ache, this fear deep inside her, what he had meant? Because it was real. And it hurt. She clutched her arms about her and hugged the pain like a friend. She wanted it to hurt.

With Jonathan it had been all parties and presents, a whirlwind of fun after the shock and hurt of her parents' sudden death. He had made her feel alive again, sweeping her off her feet in a round of pleasure. Had he counted on that vulnerability? Had he been that cynical? She didn't bother to answer her own questions. It didn't matter any more. All that mattered was that the children were safe. That Nick was safe.

She peered out into the beam of light thrown by the lights of the van, hoping she might catch a glimpse of him. But there was nothing; while she had been searching for the glasses, checking the food supply, he had had plenty of time to swim way beyond the headlights' beam and she shivered to think of him out there, in the darkness.

'Nick!' She called again into the darkness. 'I love you, damn it. Do you hear me? I love you.' And then she whispered the words over and over as, holding his shirt to her face, she sank to her knees.

How long would it take him to reach the island? How long to return with the children? She turned her torch on her watch. Three-thirty. It would start to get light in a little more than an hour. He couldn't possibly make it back before the police arrived. Could he?

Hugging his shirt to her chest, she waited, straining for the slightest sound in the darkness. But what had seemed until then like absolute silence was full of small night-time noises. The barest movement of air disturbing the leaves.

Tiny mammals moving about in the undergrowth. A vole plopping into the water, making her jump and disturbing a sleeping duck so that it fluttered its feathers indignantly before settling down again. Then one of the dogs up at the farm began to bark.

Behind her the sky began to lighten almost imperceptibly, but the lake remained dark against the western sky. And still she remained, listening for the tell-tale sound of an oar, or a swimmer, or a cry for help in the darkness. She was cold. But it wasn't the damp mist that was chilling her to the bones. It was fear.

'Oh, Nick,' she murmured. 'Oh, my darling, where are you?'

The black outline of the island had begun to stand out against the water when she first thought she heard something and leapt to her feet.

Small watery sounds that might have been oars, or might just have been the water lapping at the shore. Or might just have been the result of wanting to hear something.

'Cassie?' Joe, still in his pyjamas, but wearing his wellingtons and an anorak, came up behind her. 'What are you doing? Where're Mike and Nick?' He rubbed his eyes and then spotted that the dinghy was gone. 'They've gone sailing at night! Without saying a word. Well, of all the rotten things to do . . .'

Cassie sniffed, rubbed something damp from a cheek chilled as the breeze began to rise with the coming dawn. 'I know. Rotten. But you'll get your turn, Joe. When you're bigger.' Her voice sounded over-bright, horribly false, but Joe didn't seem to notice anything wrong and when she sank back to the decking he settled down beside her. 'It's going to be a long day, sweetheart; don't you think you should go back to bed?'

'I'll wait for Mike.' Then he lifted his head. 'What's that?'

It *was* something. Something quite close. Then she saw it. The dinghy, with two figures, their backs to the shore as they tugged on the oars, working hard, but not quite in rhythm. It had to be Mike and Sadie. They'd given up, come back. Perhaps they even hoped that they wouldn't have been missed.

Joe saw them too and leapt up. 'They've had to row,' he crowed. 'They've had to row!'

Cassie stood up, but more slowly, as something like ice crystallised around her heart. Mike and Sadie were safe. But where was Nick?

Oh, darling. You should have waited. At least long enough for me to tell you that you were right, to tell you that I love you. That I would trust you with my life.

The dinghy bumped against the end of the jetty and Joe shot forward to grab the rope and tie it up. And that was when she saw him. He was in the water, swimming lazily after the dinghy as if there were nothing in the world to worry about. As if she weren't breaking up into little pieces inside . . .

'What the devil did you think you

were doing?' she demanded, sweeping past the startled children and standing over him as he swam up to the side of the jetty. 'How dare you do something so stupid, so irresponsible?' Nick had propped his elbows on the wooden boards and was looking up at her with an expression that if she had stopped to think about it might have been described as satisfaction. Possibly even slightly smug. But he remained in the water and as the sky turned a pearly pink with the dawn, turning the silken skin of his shoulders to a golden blush, her mouth dried. She loved him so much, wanted him so much and instead of telling him she was standing there berating him like some fish-wife.

'Have you finished?' he asked, rather too gently for her raw nerves.

'No, I most certainly have not finished, Nick Jefferson. Have you any idea what I've been through?'

Nick glanced at Mike and Sadie. 'You see, I *told* you she wouldn't shout at you.'

'No one's going to shout at anyone,' Cassie shouted. 'But if you think I'm going to keep quiet after all you've put me through — '

'Mike, why don't you and Sadie go and get into some dry clothes?' Nick said. 'We'll be along in a minute or two.'

'Yes, quickly,' Cassie said, trying hard to hold onto a sudden need to shout very loudly indeed. 'And you, Joe. Go, now.'

Mike glanced at Nick uncertainly, knowing that he should say something, wanting to say something. 'Not now, Mike.' And with the smallest gesture of his head Nick let him go. Relieved, the boy scrambled from the dinghy, giving Sadie a hand.

'Now, my darling, I'm entirely at your disposal,' he said, when they were quite alone. 'What exactly did you want to say to me?'

She swung around to face him and exploded. 'Get out of the water, Nick Jefferson — '

'You're sure?'

'I've got a few things to say to you — no, actually quite a lot of things, and I'm certainly not doing it with you down there and me up here.'

'Whatever you say, sweetheart.' He put his hands flat on the decking and pulled himself out of the water. Too late, Cassie realised why he had stayed there as he reached for his jeans and tugged them on, totally unconcerned that he was buck naked. And all of a sudden Cassie saw red.

'Don't you 'sweetheart' me,' she said, flinging a fist at his shoulder as he bent to pick up his shirt, beating at his chest with her hands as he straightened, took a step back. 'You're an idiot, Nick Jefferson,' she said, following him. 'Going off like that without a word. Have you no consideration? Don't you know I've been worried to death about you out there in the dark?'

'But I thought you wanted the children back.'

'I did. But you could have missed them in the dark . . . you could have got

312

lost . . . you could have — ' Her voice broke on a tiny sob as her fists finally came to a stop against his cold, damp skin.

'I could have been eaten by one of Nessie's relations . . . ' he offered, the corner of his mouth tilting in a smile.

'It's not funny, Nick . . . '

'I know, love, I know,' he murmured as she gave another half-hearted blow at his chest. He caught her hands, held them, then pulled her into his arms, holding her hard for a minute against his cold, wet body. 'Would it have mattered so much to you?'

She sniffed. 'Of course it would,' she mumbled against him.

'Would it?' he demanded, pulling away, forcing her to look up at him, answer him properly.

'Of course it would, you fool,' she answered, already recovering from her fright. 'Who do you think would have driven us home if you'd killed yourself playing at being a hero?'

'You know, I'm disappointed in you,

Cassie. If that's the best you can do I might as well have stayed out there . . . but it's odd, when I was swimming out to the island I could have sworn I heard you shout something . . . '

'Maybe it was just the water in your ears,' Cassie hedged.

'Twice,' he said. 'Of course, if you're saying I'm wrong, I might just as well turn around now and swim back to that island, set up as a hermit . . . '

He reached for the waist button of his jeans, but she reached out and caught his hand. He waited. 'You'd starve in a week without someone to cook for you.'

'Quite possibly.' His eyes softened in the pearl grey of the dawn. 'Is that an offer?'

There was a long moment, a moment of acknowledgement that the past was gone and only the future mattered. 'You know it is.'

'Then say the words, Cassie. Don't hedge . . . a hedge is something you hide behind.'

'I think . . . at least . . . I'm sure . . . '

'That certain, huh?'

He wasn't going to help her out. She was going to have to do it all by herself. 'I love you, damn it. There, will that do?'

'"I love you, damn it."' He finally allowed his face to smile. 'Damn it, I love you back.'

'I love you. I love you. I love you. There. Are you satisfied?'

'Mmm. Actually, I was quite sure I heard you the first time. I just wanted you to say it to my face. What finally convinced you?'

'You . . . '

'Yes?'

'I love you. That's all. You were right when you said I'd know.' And once the difficult words were said, the rest seemed to just flow out of her. 'Knowing that you might die out there in the lake, knowing that I would have taken your place if I could, knowing that I'd never forgive myself for not having the courage to face my feelings because I was scared. Being so afraid that I would never get the chance to say all that. And realising that the whole of life is a risk, that I might be safer with my heart in a safety-deposit box, but I would be a whole lot poorer, too. All that.'

'Well, I did come back, Cassie, so you can tell me how you feel any time you like. I promise I won't get tired of hearing it.'

'I love you, Nick. And thanks to you I'm ready to take a risk on love.'

'You're sure, now?' he asked, but laughed as he said it.

She smiled and reached up and touched his cold cheek. 'Well, you know what they say, Nick — a little of what you fancy — '

'Does you good?'

'And I guess there's no point in denying the fact that I've fancied you like crazy since the first moment you walked into Beth's bookshop.'

'None whatever. It was written all over your face.' But her gasp of outrage at such blatant self-assurance was smothered by his kiss which, as the sun burst from the hills behind the lake, was sweet and tender, homage and promise.

'Oh, *gross*. They're *kissing*!'

Nick and Cassie turned to discover that they had a large and interested audience of children, and that a couple of policemen were also enjoying the view. 'Shouldn't you all be doing something useful?' Nick suggested. 'Like packing?' The little ones ran off, giggling.

'All safe, then, Mr Jefferson?' one of the policemen said.

'Oh, lord yes, I'm sorry; I should have called you straight away but — '

'But you were distracted, sir.' He grinned at Cassie. 'Quite understandable.'

'Would you like some tea?' Cassie asked quickly. 'I was just about to make some.'

'That's very kind, miss, but we won't stop, thanks all the same.' Still grinning, he turned to Mike and Sadie, who were lingering by the jetty. 'Don't you do anything like that again, now. Do you hear me?'

They nodded solemnly, and after the two men had gone Nick turned to them. 'Well?' he said. 'What have you got to say for yourselves?'

Mike stepped forward. 'I'm sorry, Aunt Cassie.'

'Me too.' Sadie looked close to tears and Cassie gathered her up and cuddled her.

'It wasn't her fault,' Mike insisted.

'Nick, will you take Sadie? I want a word with Mike.'

He glanced at her, then nodded. 'Take your time. I'll put the kettle on.'

'I found your note, Mike,' Cassie said, once they were alone. 'No one else saw it, no one else need ever see it.' The boy stared at his feet. 'You aren't to blame, you know, because your mum and dad are going through a bad patch. It's a grown-up thing, a thing that sometimes happens when people are so busy that they forget to tell one another how much they love each other. Your mother might get impatient with you, but she loves you more than you can ever know, Mike. I promise you she'll be missing you like mad.'

He looked doubtful. 'Will they split up? Some of the kids at school, their parents have split up . . . '

Cassie wasn't about to make promises that were not in her power to keep. 'I don't know, Mike. But they've had a few days together to catch up on the talking. Maybe that's all they needed. But it's their problem. Not yours.' She gave him a hug. 'Come on. Let's get some breakfast; you must be starving. Did you row all the way to the island?'

'No. We started off all right, but then the wind dropped and we were stuck out there in the middle. We fiddled about for a bit, trying to find some wind, but it was hopeless. We'd only been rowing for about ten minutes when Nick arrived.'

'Oh.'

'He wouldn't get into the boat and

help us, though. He said we'd got ourselves into a mess and we had to get ourselves out of it or how would we ever learn.'

'That's true, of course.'

'Yes. Except he wasn't exactly telling the truth, was he?'

'Wasn't he?'

'He didn't get into the boat because of Sadie.' Cassie tried to look puzzled. 'I saw him get out of the water, Aunt Cassie. He didn't have any clothes on. And Sadie's a girl. I suppose he thought she'd be embarrassed.'

Cassie couldn't think of a suitable answer right then. She was too busy being grateful he hadn't thought it necessary to question why she hadn't been.

* * *

They were having an early breakfast when they heard the sound of a car bumping down the lane and Joe rushed out to investigate. 'It's Mum and Dad,' he shouted from the gate, full of excitement. 'They've come to fetch us.'

Matt parked beside the minibus and almost before he had come to a halt Lauren was out of the car, scrambling to hug her three boys. 'Lord, but I've missed you,' she said, laughing.

'As soon as the plane landed Lauren insisted on driving straight here, instead of going home,' Matt said.

'In that case you'd better have some breakfast.' Nick suggested. 'No, stay and talk,' he said, putting his hand on Cassie's shoulder as she began to get up. 'I think I can handle a few rashers of bacon without burning them.'

'Come and see the boat, Dad,' Mike demanded. 'Nick's taught me to sail and I want to join the sailing club. Can I, Dad? Can I?'

Lauren grinned as Matt was dragged off by Mike, the other children following Pied Piper-like as they headed for the lake. 'He's nice, Cassie.'

'Yes, he is.'

Lauren didn't push it. 'I'm glad for

you. And this place is so pretty. I'd really no idea. Matt made it sound like . . . you know, all that macho men's stuff.'

'Maybe that's because he's never been here with a woman. I can recommend it.'

'It's certainly brought a glow to *your* cheeks, little sister.'

'You've got a certain glow yourself for an old lady. How was Portugal?'

'Oh, you know,' Lauren said, lying back against the grass.

'No. Tell me.'

'We had time to talk, time to relax. Time for everything. I'd forgotten what that was like. And Matt's been wonderful, couldn't do enough. Do you know a week ago I was ready to walk out and leave the lot of them?'

'No? Really?' Cassie's voice was deeply sceptical and Lauren grinned, just a touch sheepishly.

'I've been rather horrible lately. Poor Matt.'

'Mike's been suffering, too. He needs

a lot of reassurance that whatever happens you both love him.'

'I don't know what came over me.'

'It wasn't just you. You both lost sight of what marriage is all about for a little while, darling. Too much hard work, not enough fun, perhaps. All couples need time together, alone.'

'Is that right?' Lauren opened her eyes and gave her younger sister a thoughtful look. 'In that case may I make a suggestion?' Cassie looked interested. 'Why don't Matt and I stay here for a couple more days with the children,' she said, accepting a cup of coffee from Nick, 'while you two have a well-earned break?'

Nick grinned. 'Lauren, has anyone ever told you that you've got all the hallmarks of a perfect sister-in-law?'

'No, but I'm extremely susceptible to flattery.'

'In that case you won't mind if I make an alternative suggestion? Why don't you take all the children home and leave Morgan's Landing to Cassie and me?' He saw the faintest blush heat Cassie's cheeks and he took her hand, grasping it firmly in his so that she could feel just how much he loved her. 'You see, Lauren, I have this new double sleeping bag that needs field-testing and with seven children to look after there just hasn't been the opportunity . . . '

* * *

'Is Helen putting on weight?' Nick asked his brother-in-law as they waited for the cathedral organ to announce the arrival of the bride.

Graham grinned. 'It's what you might call a souvenir of Paris. But I've warned her, if it isn't a boy this time I'm giving up.'

'Dangerous things, holidays. Cassie's sister is pregnant too but in her case it's a souvenir of Portugal. I understand she's desperate for a girl.' He grinned. 'Maybe you could swop.'

'Very funny. Where are you going for

your honeymoon, Nick?' he asked meaningfully.

Before he could answer the organist played a long chord, bringing everyone to their feet. Nick turned, caught Veronica Grant's eye and she gave a slow, conspiratorial wink. He was glad she'd decided to stay with them.

Behind her were any number of lovely look-alike blondes whom he had at one time dated but who were mostly married now. One caught his eye with a look that said, This is it, Nick Jefferson; you've finally met your match and we're all here to applaud her.

Then, above the drama of Wagner's *Lohengrin*, there was another sound, a rippled murmur that was something between a gasp and a sigh, as Cassie, on Matt's arm, seemed to float up the aisle, followed by Sadie, Bethan, Emily and Alice. They were shepherded by Beth who, as matron of honour, was holding little George's hand.

Cassie handed her bouquet to Beth, then turned to Nick, her soft golden eyes sparkling as she lifted her veil. She *was* his match, he thought. In every way. It was extraordinary that for years he'd persisted in dating what he had believed to be perfect women without ever losing his heart, but the moment he'd set eyes on Cassie, who was clearly Ms Wrong from the top of her dark brown hair to the tip of her dainty feet, all five feet and three inches of her, he'd simply fallen like a ton of bricks. He'd fought it, but he hadn't had a hope.

'What is it?' Cassie whispered, her eyes widening as he continued to stare at her. 'Have I got a smudge on my nose?'

He gave the slightest shake of his head. 'Your nose is quite perfect, sweetheart, like the rest of you. I was just thinking about our honeymoon and all the fun we're going to have souvenir hunting . . . '

Then the bishop cleared his throat, indicating that it was time they gave him their undivided attention. 'Dearly beloved . . . '

Other titles in the
Linford Romance Library:

A TIME TO DANCE

Eileen Stafford

Deborah thinks that nothing exciting happens in wartime Bristol. But then the Americans arrive, preparing to fight in occupied Europe. And for Deborah, everything changes. She finds excitement when she meets Warren and falls in love. But her romantic dreams are shattered when her father sends her away to live with her aunt in Exmouth. And more heartbreak follows when she feels forced to seek refuge in London. At the end of the war — can she ever find happiness again?